STORIES AND FAIRY TALES FROM WALES

STORIES AND FAIRY TALES FROM WALES

Rob Clarke

Beattock
Books

Table of Contents

A Hundred Stories — 1

A Wedding at Dolbadarn Castle — 5

A Land of Scones and Jam — 21

The Shepherd's Wedding — 27

The Footman and the Yew Tree — 31

The Forked Tree — 37

The Fire Fairy and the old Man — 77

The Town Sweeper — 83

A Gift for the King — 87

The Girl by the Bridge — 95

Beyond the Wall — 101

Moonlight and the Lake Fairy — 109

The Squire, the Farmer, and the Undine — 113

STORIES AND FAIRY TALES FROM WALES

A Hundred Stories

The old man had been scrambling over wet, slippery rocks for over an hour before he arrived at the pool, and while not lost, the pathway was anything but well marked.

It had rained overnight and well into the morning, causing him to either wear or carry his coat, as well as a shoulder bag carrying his camera and a small bottle of water.

Time was not critical, so when he spied a dry flat rock a few feet from the pool he sat, hoping to enjoy the quiet of the bush setting. The only sound, that of the small waterfall, splashing over the rocks and then settle into the clear cold pool.

Leaning back, he found he could rest against another stone, making the break in his walk up the hill to the fort more comfortable. Pulling out his camera, he took pictures of the area for later reference, and to provide pleasant memories of the day.

What he did not realise, was that the pool was also the home of a water nymph, who was quite startled by the clicking of the camera.

Nothing would ever show on the camera images, of course, but the nymph, who was a little put-out by the intrusion, felt some fun at the old man's expense was in order. Unaware he was to become a pleasant diversion for the tiny fairy, he relaxed against the standing rock, pulled his hat down, and closed his eyes, enjoying the peaceful sounds of the waterfall.

"I can't let him become too comfortable," she smiled to herself, and blew the hat right off the old man's head. Roused from his rest, the tired traveller looked around to see where the wind had come from, then reached forward to pick up the hat, now only inches from the pool.

Looking down into the crystal-clear water, he was startled to see not just his reflection, but that of the smiling face of a tiny girl. Thinking it was a trick of the dappled light that filled the glade, he laughed at his thoughts, rubbed his eyes, put his hat back on, and settled back onto the rock to rest a little while longer.

Pleased with herself, the little fairy wondered what other tricks she could play. Few humans walked up the rocky path to the old hill fort, and it was even more rare that any stopped to rest by the pool. Perhaps it was that most who sought the history of the hill-fort were much younger, and so found the hike less of an effort than for the old man.

Noticing that his rest was nearing sleep, she thought, "we can't have him sleeping on the job," and so flying under the waterfall cupped some sparkling droplets and dropped them onto the old man's nose.

His hand brushed the first drop away, but then another and another ran down to the tip of his nose. The tiny nymph was laughing so hard she dropped all the droplets at once, splashing onto the old man's face.

Again, a little startled, the old man opened his eyes and looked around. Perhaps some water had fallen from a wet leaf overhead, he thought, reaching into this coat pocket for a handkerchief to wipe the water from his face.

Unsure how long he had been there, and though the break in the journey had been welcome, he was still many miles from the fort, so roused himself from the peaceful glade.

Now the little fairy was sad, by her pranks, her visitor was leaving, her years of sitting under the waterfall's spray had made her long for company, and yet now, by her sport, she was chasing away the first visitor for ages who had stopped by her pool.

"I can't make him stay," she thought, "but I can give him such peaceful thoughts he may stay a little longer," and so she flew above his head and shook fairy dust over his hat.

Just as he was about to stand, the strangest feelings came over him. A sort of deep peace and contentment, tinged with a longing to stay a while longer by the pool.

Looking up to see where the sun was, in order to gauge the time, the effect of the dust so powerful, he just settled back on the rock and gazed contented into the water.

Pleased with her efforts, the tiny nymph flew up and landed on the old man's shoulder. He was, of course, quite unaware of her presence. Enjoying the long waited for company, and being quite a nice fairy really, she wondered what present she could give the old man for stopping by her pool.

"He must have a great interest in the old hill fort," she thought, "why else would he entertain the long and difficult climb to reach it."

Of course, she knew all about the fort, right back to the day when the dragons escaped from the cave under the pool. They had caused such a ruckus fighting overhead, until finally, the white one, beaten in the contest, flew off to England.

"I know," she thought, smiling to herself, "I will give him a hundred stories about the place where I live, so that when he goes home, he can write them all down for lovers of fairy tales and legends of all ages."

And so she did.

A Wedding at Dolbadarn Castle

Gatherings at the castle were rare these days, wars, and feudal infighting had depleted the coffers, not to mention the loss of labour to till the soil that provided the income for the many small towns that dotted this secluded wooded valley, a two-week ride from London.

Yet a wedding, even in these troubled times, was a great enough event for the family to throw off the sackcloth, don resplendent suit and gown, bring from hidden closets scarce remnants of fine jewellery. A time, if but short, to relive a better day.

Tradition being what it was, the eldest daughter was to be first settled, then the younger, and though anxious herself to become an independent family, Catherine was delighted her sister could be courted, and now wed to a gentleman of substance, though neither a prince nor a duke. They were all off at war, or either in hiding or incarcerated.

The guest list had been carefully chosen, well scrutinised to ensure only trusted friends attended. What few men at arms remained, scanned the surrounding grounds for intruders.

It had taken days for all the guests to arrive and settle within the dark bluestone walls. They had all risked much to attend. A pledge, not only of their love for the old duke, but for all that he stood for, and against. While her father held private discussions with the heads of the families present, she, unaware, or unconcerned with the state of the country, enjoyed the time catching up with friends and cousins, planning youthful escapades for the festivities, yet all under the watchful eyes of her mother.

For a brief time, a change was evident in the castle, a warm, inviting, and vibrant air had returned. The events of the world outside the valley pushed aside, to not allow the dark clouds of war and deprivation to sully the marriage ceremony. A new family, a new beginning, and, importantly, a new political alliance.

The buildup to the festivities continued. They delivered whole sides of beef and lamb to the castle kitchen, where a dozen cooks and scullery maids cut and prepared dish after dish of solid country fare for the main feast.

This was not to be the only sumptuous providence. Many smaller gatherings took place, all leading up to the final ball and feast.

All day, the guests busied themselves, preparing, preening and powdering for the evening's grand celebration.

Politics, if only for a brief time, was back staged. Genuine friendship and honour flowed from room to room throughout the castle.

The old duke, secluded in his quarters, quietly prepared for the evening.

A gentle knock on the door preceded his favoured knight's entrance.

"I have received this note, my lord. The intent is not clear." He bowed and left the room.

Mixed feelings crowded in on the duke. The night was one to be enjoyed, not despoiled by more political intrigue.

The seal already broken, he opened the note, the seal itself half the story, the seal of the king.

It read, "Though we are not a party to this joyous occasion, please accept our delight in the marriage of your daughter to the young viscount of York. It would please us you communicate your good fortune with us at your earliest, HR."

The Duke rang the bell furiously. His retainer entering almost immediately.

"Where is the messenger?" he demanded.

"We offered him lodging, my lord, but he declined. I suppose he has lodged in the village."

"Did he speak with any of our people?" questioned the duke.

"Not as far as I am aware, my lord, but there were times when he was not under our direct surveillance."

"Damnation, there is more to this than the note," exclaimed the duke. "Find him!"

Unknown to the duke's staff, the King's messenger had in fact not left the castle, but in seclusion, hidden by a royal informant, he prepared himself to in fact take part in the marriage festivities.

The king, eager to secure support, had passed over the slight of not being consulted or indeed invited to the wedding, had in fact sent the crown prince on a secret mission, to discover the duke's loyalty, or otherwise.

Young Harry, tired of being a pawn to his father's political intrigues, was happy to escape from London, to relax and enjoy pleasant company, free from danger and with such beautiful and charming young ladies, he intended to make the most of his brief country excursion.

During the day, he had seen the daughters of the duke at play, preparing for the evening's festivities. The younger especially had caught his eye. Dynamic, feisty even, a woman after his own heart, her fine figure matched to a quick wit and charm. Secreted behind the double wall, he watched, noting all the preparations.

His brief was clear, determine the duke's influence, and as best he could, his loyalty to the crown, then report back with all haste.

The balance of power in the land in such a state of flux, even a week, could swing the outcome of the crown.

London, however, was a long way from Snowdon, and having prepared himself for the principal task, young Harry was not as much concerned with the crown as with the duke's youngest daughter.

Nestled on a small knoll above the village, the castle was well defended, and though modest in size, well fortified. The duke had ensured that attack by land would be difficult, with earthen mounds barring the way of would-be attackers, and a waterborne approach unthinkable.

Snowdon, to the south, loomed over the valley. Any force attempting a southern route would need the determination of a Hannibal.

Harry was determined to meet the duke's youngest daughter, and despite the fears of his confident, he had devised a plan.

Unable to reveal his true identity to the duke and the assembled guests, he planned to seek admission as a travelling minstrel. The duke, on hearing the request of a musician to perform at the wedding, greeted the concept warmly, with no risk to the proceedings perceived. As an act of good faith, the minstrel's contact suggested he play privately for the duke's youngest daughter, and it would be on her recommendation whether he played for the guests, or no. With all the staff fully occupied with the preparations, he agreed, thinking it may well keep his somewhat exuberant daughter occupied.

The prince was indeed a polished performer, having spent time in both Germany and France, where, learning the finer points of the Lute, was tutored in subtle aspects of ballads and love songs.

A lute, secretly sourced, was brought to the prince, and he, disguised, was escorted by the royal confident through the castle, to a secluded garden overlooking the lake. There, sitting somewhat impatiently, the duke's beautiful young daughter, who would rather have been making mischief among the guests, than vetting some itinerant musician. Still, it was a diversion, and as she studied the approaching figure, his handsome form softened her attitude.

After a brief introduction by the prince's escort, the two were soon alone. The warmth of the late morning sun would allow the prince all the time needed to carry out his plan.

It was certainly not expected that a musician would actually address the duke's daughter, so initially the prince played some pleasant welsh tunes, but then, moving closer, he changed to play and sing seductive French love songs. Her French, though lacking, the intent in the melodies, was unmistakable. With her face now blushed, though not from the sun, she sat transfixed, motionless except for her eyes, which now looked into the musician's face.

His smile at the end of the song hung in the air, as if waiting for a response, but he was in no mood to lose the upper hand.

"Was my lady well pleased with the performance?" His eyes looking straight into hers.

Shifting awkwardly, she was unsure how to answer this forward young man. His eyes sparkled in anticipation, her rosy cheeks all the answer he needed.

"I will discuss the matter with my father," was all she could say, and then continued, "Still, you could play a little more." Her tone, though imperious, fooled neither.

Moving closer, now only feet away from the beautiful girl, the prince at first fussed with his instrument, as if luring her deeper into his trap. Unashamed, he studied her face, while she, in return, fidgeted on the seat. Clearly attracted to the young man, but out of her depth in such a situation.

Again, the prince played, not just on the strings of the lute, but also on the heartstrings of the duke's daughter. Now seated beside her, the strings at last silent, but the music played on.

"I'm not quite who I appear to be, my lady. Though my musical art is in full bloom, I am of noble birth, and desire to, with appropriate approval of course, court you. Would that be agreeable?"

Her head was now swimming. The warmth of the day, the seductive strings of the lute, and the handsome face of the young musician, all too much to take in.

"Perhaps I will speak with you again good sir, now, I fear I have to take my leave, good day to you," and with that, rose form the seat, and headed, as quickly as decorum allowed, into the castle.

A little bemused, but otherwise satisfied, the prince sat in the garden until his confident arrived, who, with consternation, pleaded with the prince to retire to a more secure abode.

"My prince, I pray you leave the castle with all haste before we are exposed."

"Good Sir knight, your concern for our safety is a comfort, and yes, it may well be prudent we seek other lodging before the festivities."

"What said the duke's daughter, my prince?"

"Not with her words did she entertain my presence, but her heart surely leapt from her breast with encouragement."

"But how will the duke respond to the king's note?"

"The note broods within the duke, unsure of my father's intent. That is my quest, and tonight, through his daughter agreeing to my presence, I intend to draw out the answer. Let's away to the other side of the lake."

With practised ease, the two made their way out of the castle walls unseen, except by one.

Restless from her encounter with the young minstrel, her mind and heart in turmoil over his strange utterance, she lounged against an upper window, gazing down towards the water.

Suddenly, she noticed two figures quietly leaving the grounds, making their way, not towards the village, where one might abide, but down the slope to the water's edge, where she lost sight of them in the trees.

The stature of one, she was sure, was that of the young musician.

Down at the water's edge, a strong wind, which caused such a tempest, thwarted the escape.

"I must return to the castle, my prince. The duke will have already noted my absence."

"Go, friend, there is shelter enough here for me until this evening."

"God's grace keep you, my prince."

Riveted now to the window, the duke's daughter scanned the way from the lake, and in one-half hour, one returned, and being eager not to be noticed, returned into the castle via the North gate.

"He has to be a trusted employee," she thought, "to have such unchecked access to the castle." He seemed familiar to the girl, but the hooded coat kept a sure identification from her.

Her thrill of intrigue and adventure overcame her good sense, and so rather than prepare for the evening's festivities, she changed into men's attire, so as not to be noticed, and made her way to the north gate.

Unsure where she was going, or what she may find, her heightened intrigue over the young minstrel drove her on, across the lawns and into the heavily wooded outer grounds of the castle.

Often, she had walked the path down to the water's edge, but now, attempting to perhaps catch the plotters unawares, she took a stumbling, untrodden passage through the trees and rocks.

Her foot landed on a dead branch. The snap resounded like a musket report through the stillness of the forest.

She froze, had her passage through the woods discovered, no fleeing deer gave her presence away, yet she dare not proceed until she thought it safe.

Why was she following him? She was unsure who he actually was, and should she confront another? What then? The afternoon long gone, she ought to have been safe within the confines of the castle.

So much had happened. Was she ready for the outcome? Still, she had to know. Carefully climbing over moss covered rock and branch, she made her way to the water's edge.

Alone, and unwilling to light a fire, the prince patiently waited in a makeshift shelter, some twenty feet from the windswept water's edge.

His keen hearing detected the cracking of a branch, his hand soon at his sword. He was not just alone; his whole quest could now hang by a thread.

Crouching behind heavy thickets, he waited and watched. Soon, a slightly built figure appeared.

"Certainly no woodsman," he thought to himself as the intruder slipped and slid down the moss-covered rocks.

Clearly, the intruder was searching for him, and as such was no friend, but an adversary.

Unfamiliar with the terrain, the intruder missed a footing and stumbled past the prince's hiding place, arms sprawled out over the muddy earth.

Sensing his opportunity, the prince leapt from his cover and pinned his foe to the ground. "Move and it will be your last!" his sword menacingly poised above his captive's back.

"Spare me, spare me!" cried the fallen foe. Startled, the prince recognised the voice as being female, even to the point he suspected it was that of the duke's young daughter, who but an hour ago sat enraptured with his singing. What was she doing here?

"Stand and face me!" he demanded.

Dragging herself from the forest floor, stunned and frightened, she turned to face her attacker. His sword still drawn, the prince drew back the hood covering the head of his captive. No rugged warrior faced him, in fact, no warrior at all, but indeed, it was the duke's daughter.

Her hair in disarray, her complexion drawn with fear. Trembling, she stood before him.

"What brings you here, lady Catherine? These woods are filled with all manner of hurts for a duke's daughter." Putting his sword away, he took her trembling hands.

Slowly the shock and fear subsided, and as she looked into his face, the eyes, those sparkling eyes, she recognised who it was standing before her.

"And what business does a minstrel have lurking in the duke's woodland?"

He ignored the question, busying himself cleaning the water and mud from her face and hands. His touch was gentle and caring, as would a lover. He eased her down onto a large flat rock, and there they sat, as they had sat just an hour before, yet now with no musical distraction, without pretence of any kind.

"I saw you leave the castle with another, then only one returned. Who are you? What are you doing here?" This time, she wanted an answer.

"I told you, my lady, I was not from common stock, and neither I am. My purpose here, I cannot at this time disclose, but be assured, it is not with any malice or evil intent I desire access to the castle. What I can tell you is that all you need to know, you will know tonight."

"And what of me? What would your intentions be?"

"Ah," he looked lovingly into her eyes, and held her hands tight, "you were not part of the original plan, and yet now, if I am not strong of will, my capture of your heart and hand, would be my only goal."

He drew her close, as if to kiss her, receiving no resistance to his advances.

Releasing his hands to hold her waist, she raised hers to stroke his face.

"This will never end well, sir. My father would never allow an unknown gentleman to have my hand, or any part of me."

He smiled, "Leave your father to me, my lady. My charms extend much further than you might imagine." And with that, he kissed her lips.

"Still, we cannot tarry here my sweet, you will be missed, and a search will disrupt the wedding plans, and I- I have to, as your minstrel, play my part tonight."

Standing, he raised her up beside him, and taking her hand, led her back to the edge of the woods before the castle walls.

"My plan is to amuse the guests during the feast, and in that, discover all I need to know, by subtly, and not force. It may cause a little disruption, but I pray the outcome will suit all." He smiled once more, and with a kiss on her forehead, he prompted her to walk back to the castle, then turned and slipped back into the gloom of the trees.

Catherine, as quickly as she could, crept back to her quarters, her absence noted, but not yet escalated to concern for her whereabouts. Her ladies-in-waiting fussed and questioned her absence.
"I felt a little flushed, and needed some cool air," was all she would answer, her face radiant and eyes sparkling.

Now, in the early evening, the castle was abuzz with wedding preparations. Trestles groaned under the abundance of food of all manner. Ladies in their finest gowns were preparing to make their entrances into the grand hall.

The duke surveyed the hall from his private window and smiled. All was ready, a night to forget the issues of the kingdom, the castle locked down to keep out all who would, or could, disrupt the festivities.

Entering quietly and unnoticed, the minstrel tarried near the kitchen, as befitted his station. The notion pleased him, as he had not eaten that day since leaving his men on the other side of the lake.

He was to have no part in the actual wedding, a closed affair, held in the castle chapel. During one security check, he drew an odd look of concern, but a powerful arm drew the enquirer on to other parts. A fleeting glance between the prince and his father's faithful knight, the heightened tension clear in their faces. So much to play for, the risks equalling the reward.

A hush lay over the castle, like the morning mist which daily blanketed the lake. Even the kitchen cooks and serving maids paused, hoping to catch a word from the chapel.

Secure in the hallway, secluded in the bluestone's dark passage, the prince, anxious to have done with his father's task, would, however, be faithful to the end, no matter what the consequences. His mind racing as to the details of the plan. Would the duke respond as hoped, would the festivities plummet into chaos, and what of the lovely Catherine, would his chance at love be also dashed, should all go badly for him.

He held no fear as to his own safety. The token, given to him by his father, should quiet any danger, except that from lesser men, who, he hoped, would not be in attendance.

The blast of trumpets roused him from his thoughts. Soon the play would begin, soon all would have to be revealed. But not too soon. The timing had to be perfect.

In the great hall, the festivities had begun, sturdy trestles placed in a large U. The duke at the head, flanked by the groom's parents on his left, and to the right, the bride and groom. Lady Catherine seated next to her sister.

A jolly mood prevailed, toasts made and drunk, rich food consumed in abundance. It was indeed a merry night.

"Catherine," the duke called to his daughter, "where is your minstrel? Let us have some jolly songs!"

"I will fetch him, father," came her reply. Eager to see his face again, but in trepidation as to the outcome of his quest, she summoned a servant, instructing her to fetch the minstrel into the hall.

Pacing a little in excitement, the prince was relieved when the girl appeared and asked him to follow her to the waiting guests. "Play well, sir, the duke is not to be disappointed." She looked at him sternly.

From the gloom of his post near the kitchen, the bright lights of the hall caused him to blink, the rush of sound and colour filled his head.

Quickly, he glanced around the hall, over a hundred in attendance, but his eyes were only for two, the duke, and his daughter.

With assumed humility, he approached the head table. "Young man, I hear you are quite artful. Let us see if your efforts well meet my daughter's recommendation. Some merry tunes, I pray, to suit the joyous night."

"My lord, may my fingers and throat provide you with much pleasure."

With that, he sat on a stool in front of the head table, such that he could turn and face most of the guests, and with a slight nod to Lady Catherine, he bent to play.

Opening with some popular Welsh ballads, the prince entered fully into the occasion, and, to impress his host, sang also some German folk songs, which solicited much acclaim from the assembled guests.

He paused in his playing. The waiting staff brought in the next course. Roast duck on platters filed past him. He waited for the clatter to abate, during which he studied the guests, looking for a familiar face, either friend or foe. Often his gaze rested on Catherine, but then, returning to the task at hand, fixed his eyes on the duke, who, busy with his guests, scarcely noticed the young minstrel.

With the duck being consumed with relish, a quiet came over the hall, to which the duke responded.

"Minstrel, some more delightful sounds I pray, a sovereign for your troubles, should you please us."

With a smile and a nod, the player began a serenade. With dexterity and poise, the graceful music flowed through the air, some even stopping to listen, so taken were they with his skill.

"Now is the time," he thought, "Please God for the right outcome." And with that silent prayer, he put his hands once more to the strings, but this time, no sweet ballad came from his lips, instead the hateful sounds and words of the rebel's anthem!

The hall plunged into silence. The duke leapt to his feet. "Stop, stop you vile wretch!" he yelled at the minstrel. "How dare you disgrace us with such an insult to the King's loyal subjects. Guards, bear the wretch hence!"

Shouts and angry looks now directed towards the minstrel, who, at the duke's outburst, sprang to his feet. Catherine, wide eyed, stood trembling, holding tight to the table lest she faint away. Her new love disgraced, her loyalty to her father and king torn by her love for the young man.

Castle guards, led by the duke's knight, surrounded the prince, powerful arms pinned him in their grasp. Then, as the tumult reached its peak, with threats of incarceration and beatings filling the air, the Knight called for order.

"My lord, friends, please be at peace, and I will attempt to explain all."

"What!" yelled the duke, "are you also a party to this disgrace, you, who have been at my side for years, a traitor?"

"No, my lord, I am, and always have been, your loyal servant and knight to the king, and it is in his name I crave your indulgence."

Slowly, the duke and guests calmed and resumed their places. The guards still held the minstrel tight in their arms.

"My good lord, do you remember the note from the king, lately received, which caused you so much consternation?"

"Yes, go on!" The duke still visibly upset.

"Well, as we all know, the country is fraught with infighting and insurrection, and despite my lord's longstanding support for the crown, His Majesty, as a prelude to rid north Wales of renegades, sought a clear sign of your allegiance, to which I was sworn to secrecy. He, unwilling to take your servant's advice, dispatched an emissary, to view at first hand my lord's love for the king, or no."

"Where is this man, that I may swear my allegiance to the king!" the duke demanded.

"I am here, sir," replied the minstrel.

"You, an itinerant musician, why would the king entrust such a task to the likes of you?"

"Indeed, my lord," replied the knight, "this is the man, but may I assure you, he is of no common blood."

The stern face of the duke drilled into the musician's eyes. "Then, who are you, sir?"

"If we could release the minstrel, my lord, he himself will declare all," the knight attempting to maintain some order.

"Very well, unhand the musician."

The guards grudgingly released their grip, and stood back a pace, but not so far that they could not catch him again in quick time.

"Good sir, if I may, via your good and faithful knight, give you this token for inspection, you will then understand well enough who I am." And with that, the prince took off the ring, and handed it to his confidant, to carry directly to the duke.

The ring now in his hands, the duke's eyes wide, knowing at once the name and title of the owner. It was the ring of the prince of wales, the eldest son of the king himself, who, so recently, was manhandled as a villain.

"I apologise for the deception, and late furore, but the king charged me to have, and with all certainty, confirm that which you have always shown, complete loyalty to the crown."

"This night of joy, which I have sadly, but willingly, disrupted, I did in the king's name, who's name I also bear, and will at length, so council my father of your enduring love for his person and estate."

A hush came over the guests, for there in their midst, the king's son, who but a few minutes past, was one they would cause great mischief.

"I will, in private, discuss more fully with you the reason for the subterfuge and pain I have caused, which, when you are fully appraised, will forgive me, I'm sure."

"As is your pleasure, my prince." The duke replied, "knight, escort our prince to the table. What minor inconvenience has now taken place is much removed by the presence of the king's son at our celebration. Let the festivities resume!"

All eyes were now on the minstrel, but now seated at the duke's right hand. Food and drink soon fetched for the royal guest.

The prince again surveyed the assembly, this time as his subjects, and he as their crown prince. Slowly, he scanned the room, all the while in conversation with thc duke and his party. Then, at length, he could no longer avoid her. With a smile and sparking eyes, he stared at Catherine, a look noted by all.

She, for her part, sat still, while hundreds of eyes, first at the prince, and then in her direction, gazed intently, seeking for a clue as to this clear and unmistakable bond.

"If I may speak to the gathering, my kind host, I have somewhat to say, both to them, and issue a request to you."

"My house is yours, my prince. Speak on."

Standing, the duke called for order, and remaining standing, turned to the prince.

"Friends, the Prince of Wales demands your attention." And with that, all the gathering rose to their feet, along with the prince.

"Please, good friends one and all, be seated, and my generous host, much thanks for your kindness. My father, in a brief and obscure note to the duke, referred to this happy wedding, and it is indeed my great pleasure to have been able to give my own regards to the couple. I wish you both great happiness and prosperity, both in my name, and in the king's name."

"And, guests of my host, in time the fruits of this strange happening will become clear, but until then, I pray you all will be content to wait until all is revealed."

Then, turning to the duke, and yet continuing speaking to all, he continued. "Good, my host, on this auspicious night, one more thing I would desire from you, and I pray you will not refuse me."

"Anything, my prince, even to my castle and estate," the duke replied.

"Keep your castle and your lands, good friend. I have no desire for them, but something dearer to your heart that I crave."

The duke quizzically looked at the prince. What could he desire more than castle and lands?

"What then, my prince, would you have?"

"The hand of your daughter, Catherine."

Catherine and her mother both swooned, as ladies do, while the whole assembly burst into cheering and applause.

The duke was speechless, his daughter to be queen of England, his status elevated to a level unimagined. Still, where there are boons, there is often a sting in the tail, but here, on this night, no thought of consequences could be imagined.

Catherine, now recovered, was brought to her father, and with the three standing before the assembled guests, he joined in hand, the prince, and Catherine.

"Take her, my prince. May God Almighty guard and prosper you both, and make the crown of England most secure."

Cheering again broke out, from the greatest to the least, throughout the castle.

The knight, standing back, basked in the venture's success. His allegiance to both King and duke secure, his honour maintained, his friend and confidant soon to wed, and a more safe and peaceful land for all.

A Land of Scones and Jam

Once upon a time, right at the end of a very long valley, there was a small kingdom.

The tops of the mountains that enclosed the kingdom were so high and covered with snow no-one had ever been to see what was on the other side, no-one even thought anything might be there at all.

All the people in the land were contented and happy. The king was both wise and kind, so there wasn't a single person who had ever thought of leaving and no-one had ever arrived from anywhere else.

A beautiful clear stream ran through the middle of the valley, fed from springs and the melting snow from high behind the town. The water had never run out and there were never any people getting sick in the entire region.

As the children in the land grew up, they built another house or moved into one when the old folk who had lived there died. There was no radio, no newspapers, and certainly no television. In fact, the only way anyone knew what was happening was when they all went to the market on Wednesday to buy their vegetables and fruit. There they would chat and discuss the weather, who had just had a baby or got married or died.

The kingdom stayed this way year after year after year.

There was no army in the kingdom as there was no-one to fight with, so the king only had six soldiers who always dressed in colourful uniforms to match the King's flag that fluttered above the castle when the cool breeze blew down the valley.

It was a modest castle. There was no moat or draw-bridge, as he didn't need one.

Most days, the king would walk out of the castle and down to the town. There, people were always happy to see him and were as polite as could be.

The king liked tea with scones and jam, so he would always stop at the baker's shop, where the baker would greet the king and show him to a very nice table next to the window so the king could see all the people going past.

The baker's wife would bring out a pot of tea, placing it right in front of the king.

As the people of the town walked past the window, they would all look in, nod politely and walk on, but no-one said good morning or in fact anything at all.

You see, the king didn't like loud sounds and enjoyed peace so much it was almost the quietest town you could ever imagine. Even the gurgling stream that ran past tried hard not to make too much noise.

At precisely ten o'clock, the king would leave the baker's shop and walk back to the castle. He always left a little extra money on the table to cover the cost of the tea.

Inside the walls that surrounded the king's house, there was a large garden. The king had three gardeners, one who tended the flowers and the fruit trees, one who looked after the vegetable garden, which was around the back near the kitchen, and one who mowed and trimmed the lawns.

When he returned from his tea and scones, the king would walk through the garden and if it was a Monday, he would snip off a rose, if it was Tuesday, he would take a Lilly and so on through the week, each day a different flower as the king didn't have any favourites, he loved them all.

The gardener who mowed the lawns would wait until the king had left the castle for his morning tea before starting his work and then stop at precisely ten minutes past ten, as then the king would soon be in earshot of the sound coming from the garden.

One day, the gardener who mowed the lawn became ill and so for some time, the grass grew untrimmed and was soon some inches high.

The other gardeners were too busy doing their own job, so although they noticed they didn't have time to do the other gardener's work. Because the king had never seen the sick gardener mowing the grass, he just thought it had always been that way so when he saw how high it had become, he called for the vegetable and flower gardeners to explain, as he always saw them busy in the grounds.

"Why is the grass growing?" He asked.

"The other gardener is sick, your majesty, and we are too busy to do any more work."

"But I have seen no one cutting the grass. How was it done?" the king asked again.

"Well Sir, every day when you go for your walk into the town to have your tea and scones, the other gardener would take his mower and trim the grass, he would always stop before you returned so the noise would not bother you."

The king shook his head in wonder. "I will go and see him," said the king, "and I will take him some fresh scones. That will make him feel better."

The very next day instead of sitting by the window in the baker's shop, the king had the baker and the baker's wife prepare a large tray of hot scones and then along with his six soldiers, they all marched to the house of the sick gardener.

A soldier knocked on the door and when the gardener's wife looked out, she was startled to see the soldiers, the king, the baker, and his wife all standing outside.

Brushing her hair, she ran to the door and curtsied to the king.

"I hear my gardener is unwell, so we have brought the very best scones to help him recover," the king said with a smile.

"Please come in, your majesty," the gardener's wife replied.

Soon the tiny house was full of people. The king sat near the stove, as the morning was a little crisp.

"Would you care for a cup of tea, your majesty?" asked the gardener's wife.

As it was the time when the king would have had his tea in the baker's shop, her offer pleased him.

One soldier suggested he take the scones into the gardener before they went cold and walked through the house to where the gardener sat in bed. "The king was worried you have not been tending the grass and has brought you some fresh scones to make you well." He said, setting the enormous plate of scones on a small table near the bed. He turned and left the room.

The gardener, surprised at seeing a soldier come into the bedroom, was even more surprised to see all the scones piled high on the plate.

After a few days of being unwell, the gardener was in fact feeling much better, and as the smell of the fresh scones wafted up, he smiled and took one from off the plate.

Next to the scones, the baker had placed a jar of strawberry jam and next to that, a tub filled to the brim with fresh cream.

The gardener took the knife and piled jam and cream onto the scone, which he gulped down. He was about to have another one when he thought if a soldier had brought the scones into him, then the king himself must be in the house.

The scone had been delicious but as there were too many for him to eat he got out of bed, pulled on his dressing gown, picked up the tray and walked back to the kitchen where he saw the room packed with people and the king sipping tea by the fireplace. Walking to the table, he placed the scones right in front of the king.

Looking up at the gardener, the king smiled and exclaimed to all in the room, "See, I told you all that a scone and jam will fix nearly anything." The king was pleased the gardener had not eaten all the scones and took one off the plate, covered it with jam and cream and with one bite ate it whole.

All the people in the room watched as the king reached and took another scone. This time, he took two bites before it was all eaten. With a most cheerful smile, he looked around at the kitchen full of people and then back at the plate of scones. "I think we should all have a scone," the king suggested, "if they have cured my gardener, and I feel very well, then we all should feel better by having one each."

Being polite, no-one rushed to the table, but everyone soon had a scone smothered with strawberry jam and cream. The gardener's wife had been busy making tea for everyone, so the king made sure there was one scone left on the plate for her.

"My goodness," exclaimed the king, "it is ten o'clock. I must be going." He got up, and as he always did, he left some money on the table for the tea. The soldiers wiped off any of the jam and cream from their lips and formed up outside.

Everyone followed the king back to the castle. The baker and his wife took the empty plate and tubs back to their shop.

Sitting alone together in the kitchen, the gardener, and his wife wondered why the king would have come to their house, but both knew it would be a tale they would tell all their days.

Next day when the king returned from his tea and scones, the gardens were all neat and trim. The grass had been cut, and the edges were as sharp as a knife could make them.

Walking through the entrance, he noticed the three gardeners talking to each other and called them over. "Well done, you three," he said. "I am so pleased to see not just the flowers and the trees all neat, but the grass is as fine as I have ever seen it, and all because of my scones." He smiled a warm smile and walked into the castle.

The gardeners all looked at each other and wondered what on earth the king could have meant, but they were much too polite to ask.

Now it has never been proved that eating scones and jam could fix nearly anything, but in every house in the kingdom, no-one ever had tea without fresh scones with jam, and oh yes, a lot of cream as well.

The Shepherd's Wedding

A long time ago, a shepherd boy was in love with a miller's daughter; they had to meet in secret as her father saw the boy as too poor to court his daughter.

Every day, the lad led his sheep up the nearby mountain to pasture; it was a long walk, but the sheep were safe from prowling wolves. Each day, he passed a small waterfall fed by a spring higher up the mountain. Often he would stop to drink from the pool below the waterfall, but this day the waterfall had stopped, and the pool had dried up.

It had been quite a while since a fierce storm had blown down a large tree that now blocked the hole from where the spring fed the tiny stream.

With the spring not able to feed the waterfall, the ground around the tree became sodden and the grass lush for some distance down the hill from the spring. There the young shepherd let his sheep feed on the grass, but not so high as to have them get stuck in the sodden earth.

The boy did not realise something connected the dried-up waterfall to the lush pasture higher up the mountain, but one day as he was leading his sheep passed the dried pool, he heard crying. Stopping to investigate, the sound seemed to come from a hole deep in the rocks behind where the waterfall fell. He looked and looked but could see nothing. After a while the sheep strayed, so he left off his search, and, gathering his flock, continued up to the pasture.

The next day he heard the crying again. This time he called out, "Are you all right?" He couldn't see anyone, but as he was alone, felt he could speak. The crying stopped, and as he looked hard into the darkness of the rocks, a flash of blue appeared and flew right up in front of his eyes.

Startled, he rubbed his eyes, thinking the sun had affected his sight; but then, when he looked again, the blue light was still there; and, when he stared, there in front of him was a tiny girl, a fairy.

"Why are you crying?" he asked.

The fairy looked at him with a very sad face but said nothing.

"Was it something I have done?"

She shook her head.

"Then why are you so sad?"

The fairy flew around the pool and up to where the water used to flow over the rocks, making the beautiful little waterfall.

"Is it because the water has stopped?" He exclaimed. The tiny nymph flew back to him and nodded excitedly.

"How is it I can hear you crying, but you cannot speak?" He looked at the tiny girl, who just seemed to shrug her shoulders, and then looked sadder than before.

"I have to go now, but I will try to see why the water has stopped, OK?"

A smile came onto the fairy's face and she bobbed up and down in front of him, her eyes now sparkling. She stayed hovering in the same spot as he turned, gathered his sheep, and walked further up the mountainside.

With his sheep all content eating the lush grass, he remembered his promise to the fairy and walked around the area to see what may have stopped the flow of water. Leaving the sheep, he went higher, finding the ground even more soft and boggy until he came to where a large tree had fallen. Water flowed all along and under the trunk of the tree, oozing out onto the ground; but none went into the old course of the stream.

Realising it was the fallen tree that had stopped the flow, he found a sturdy branch and levered the tree away from the source of the spring. After about an hour, he had moved the tree enough so that the water flowed once more into the tiny stream.

With his sheep still contented, he sat on the log, pleased with his work and, being able to keep his promise to the fairy, he played on his whistle while watching the water now run back down the hill to where the fairy lived.

That night he told his beloved all that had happened, but the tale of his exploits and finding a fairy did not make her happy. Her father had found out they were still meeting and would have her confined to the mill to stop any talk of a marriage to the poor shepherd.

The next morning as he led his sheep passed the fairy's home, the waterfall poured over the rocks, and now the pool below was full to overflowing. When she saw him, she flew to where he stood and, flying right up to him, kissed him on the nose.

When she moved back, she realised the shepherd was not happy; the fairy gave him a concerned look, in her way, asking him what troubled him. The boy sat on a stone near the edge of the pool and told the fairy all that the miller had said.

The little fairy thought for a while, then, smiling, flew back behind the waterfall. Returning with a gold sovereign, she placed it on the stone next to the shepherd.

Time and time again, she made the journey behind the waterfall until a pile of gold coins sat on the rock beside the lad. The fairy flew up to him as before and kissed his nose once more.

The shepherd, amazed, thanked the nymph over and over. He was now the richest man in the county. The first thing he did was to buy the entire mountain where the fairy lived. The miller now saw the lad differently, which was sad, as the only difference was that he was now rich and not poor.

They soon held a grand wedding with many of the townsfolk attending, especially those who were poor.

The shepherd and his new wife climbed the hill to the waterfall. Pulling out his whistle, the shepherd played for the water nymph, who, when she heard the sweet sounds, came out to greet the newlywed couple.

Flying to the pair first, she kissed the miller's daughter on the nose, then flying to the shepherd, landed on his shoulder and kissed him on the ear, whispering a secret only he could know.

For years and years, the shepherd would come back to the pool and spend time with the water nymph; he would play for her, she would sit on his shoulder, the sparkling spring water flowing over the rocks and down into the pool.

The Footman and the Yew Tree

Long ago, there were two kingdoms that had been at war with each other for many years, bringing both to the brink of ruin.

Many brave nobles and ordinary men had died, leaving not just empty coffers, but empty houses. Widows and orphans in distress filled the lands.

One of those who had fallen was an expert archer, the King's champion; who, in one terrible battle defending the bridge that led to the city, was struck down by a chance arrow loosed from the opposing army. The bridge was defended, but now the archer's son was defenceless, his wife having died at the birth of the boy.

In order to earn enough to eat, the boy cleaned the King's stables from morning to night; until one day, when the king, returning from inspecting the defences, called the boy to steady his horse while he dismounted. Looking down, he noticed a birthmark on the boy's ear.

"Whose son are you, lad?" the King asked. The boy explained who his father was, but did not know how he had died. Knowing the loyalty the archer had shown the King, even to the giving of his life, he took the boy into the castle, making him a footman, ensuring the lads keep and security.

Over time, the boy grew in stature, his fair form making him a favourite of the King's daughter.

Daily, he would lead the princess's horse while she enjoyed the freedom of the nearby woods.

One morning, while crossing a ford, the Princess's horse slipped, dislodging her. As she fell, the boy caught her and carried her to the bank of the stream. Soon they fell in love, though in secret, for he was not of noble birth.

Desperate to save his kingdom, the King sent a message to his old enemy; who, like him, was near bankruptcy. The second king had a son; spoiled, arrogant and disliked by all in the kingdom. Many feared for the future should the boy become king at his father's death.

The message sought peace through the joining of their two kingdoms, brought about by the marriage of the Princess and the Prince. The first king was not aware of the prince's flawed character, or if he did, for the sake of the kingdom, chose to see his vices in a more generous light.

Both agreed; their subjects, delighted with the cessation of warfare and suffering, enthusiastically received the news.

When the news reached the Princess and the Footman, however, they were dismayed. The Princess went to her room and would not eat; the boy walked alone in the woods; there was nothing he could do to prevent the wedding.

In a dark patch of the wood, he came upon a small graveyard. An old Yew tree spread its branches over the burial mounds, shielding those who lay under the earth.

Sitting on a tomb, the boy lamented his situation, not knowing that the grave on which he sat was that of his father.

A voice came to the boy, "An archer be, save your land and your father's name." The Yew tree bent low over the grave, one green and tender branch bowed lower than the rest, touching the soil. The voice called again to the boy, "From this, fashion a bow."

Though afraid and uncertain, the boy hearkened to the voice, and, cutting the branch from the tree, spent many weeks paring, scraping and forming the bow. Strong and subtle, the wood seemed to possess extraordinary strength. Sadly, the arrows he made were not crafted well, and try as he might, his skill did not progress as he had hoped.

In a dream, the King was warned of the young Prince's dark character, but having agreed to the union, he could not withdraw the offer. On the following night, another dream told him to hold a tournament, ensuring the right suitor would claim his daughter's hand.

Confiding the dreams to his child, she, knowing this would be the only hope of wedding the footman, agreed, suggesting the contest be that of archery.

Throughout the kingdom, young men skilled at archery presented themselves as candidates for the King's champion.

The decision to hold a contest for the Princess's hand was well received in the other kingdom, for despite his many failings, the young Prince was an expert archer. Proudly, he proclaimed he would dispatch any challenger.

A week before the contest, they had selected six archers as possible contenders; the young footman was a part of the group. They brought all before the king and his daughter. The Princess, with delight, saw her love but could not reveal her affection.

"Father, as it is my fate in the balance, may I choose your champion?" she asked. The old king agreed. Concealing her delight, she selected the footman to become the King's champion, the hand of the Princess the prize.

Daily he practised, but the arrows would not fly accurate enough to secure the victory. The day before the contest, the young Prince having arrived, the young footman sat dejected beside a stream. An old man approached. "Take these," he said. "They belonged to your father." The old man gave him twelve fletched arrows, all true. "Shoot well," the old man said and walked away.

Trying the shafts, the boy now shot with tremendous skill and accuracy, but he was still not confident. The risk of losing his love so great a burden.

Late that afternoon he returned to the graveyard and there confessed his lack of confidence. Laying the bow and arrows on the grave, he stood back. The Yew tree bent low, the branches stooped to touch the bow and the arrows.

A voice called to him, "Win the prize."

In the morning, a throng gathered to witness the competition. The two Kings sat side by side, the Princess, standing behind her father, looked on anxiously.

The two contenders faced each other, the prince dismissed the young footman contemptuously, the other in reply smiled and looked toward the Princess.

Each would have six arrows, the target some two hundred feet away. "Begin!" called the King.

The contest was over in a minute, the haughty Prince vanquished. Outraged, he demanded a rematch, but the King refused. Then, throwing his bow to the ground, stormed off the field, much to the delight of the people.

Stunned, the second king was unsure what to do. There would be no marriage between his son and the Princess, no union between the two kingdoms. Sadly, he rose and prepared to return to his country, unsure how he would relate the events of the day to his people.

After two days' travel, the King, and his son came to a narrow bridge. The rain had caused the stream to flood; the water swirled around the timbers. Slowly the King passed over, walking his horse gently so as not to disturb the structure.

The prince, still smarting from his defeat, waiting until his father was safely across, spurred his horse to a full gallop and headed for the bridge. At the first landing of the hoofs, the bridge collapsed; horse and rider swept away by the torrent, never to be seen again.

On his return, the King recounted the events to his courtiers and nobles, but with no heir, what could be done? Freed now from the advice of the spiteful Prince; the councillors, wise old men, suggested the agreed marriage still proceed. Peace between the kingdoms outweighing prideful sentiments.

They sent immediately a message, desiring the footman and Princess to travel to their kingdom to discuss a union. The young man spoke with such wisdom and compassion for the people of the land that the King and his nobles all agreed the footman would be their king.

They held a grand wedding at the border of the two countries. The old Kings crowned the young footman, now King of two peoples.

One late afternoon, not long after his crowning, he walked alone to the small graveyard carrying his bow and the arrows he had been given; sunlight shone through the branches of the Yew onto his father's grave.

Gently, he laid them on the ground.

Slowly, the tree bent low, its branches resting on the grave and the bow. When the tree raised itself back up, the bow was nowhere to be seen; it had been received back into the tree. A new branch; in the shape of a bow, budded. A soft breeze blew through the forest, waving the branches of the Yew as if to farewell the young king.

Picking up the arrows, the King returned to the palace and his queen. A new coat of arms was made, six arrows making up the central element, in honour of his father; and peace reigned throughout the land.

The Forked Tree

Walk to a strange tree

The boy had wandered through the dense woodland for hours before he spied what seemed to be a path leading higher up the steep hill. Moss-covered rocks and stunted, twisted trees seemed to guard the way, making progress difficult. Twice he had slipped, grazing his leg and bruising an arm.

He had earlier separated from his family, arguing they were going in the wrong direction. His father, knowing the boy would not come to any serious harm, let the head-strong lad make his own way to the top of the hill.

"I'll show you." He had taunted when he left his father and sister. "What fun it will be to sit on top waiting for them to arrive," he thought as off he climbed.

His mother had wisely waited in the car at the base of the hills.

The certainty of his actions soon subsided. The difficult terrain, and now, with a few cuts and bruises, denting his earlier pride. Still, for his sister to find him lost at some lower part of the climb was something he would never live down; the eternal barbs of being a bragger and a failure which would come from her at every opportunity.

With that horrid thought in mind, he tackled the climb with renewed enthusiasm. Scrambling around the edge of the hill, the track led on, but now the land seemed to open, making progress a little easier. Looking up, as until then his focus had solely been on the slippery rocks, he stopped. There in front of him was a split tree, or was it two trees joined at the base? Interesting as that was, the thing that troubled him was that the path appeared to be going through the tree, not around it. There seemed to him no good reason the makers of the path would expect travellers to squeeze through the heavy branches rather than skirting the pair of trunks.

He thought he could see the track leading on up the hill when he peered through the two limbs. Now careful not to go his own way again, he walked to the tree and pushed through to the other side.

A new World

Looking back, for one last look at where he had come from, and seeing the track winding back down the steep slope, he turned to proceed on his climb up the hill. Then, wide-eyed and fearful, he stood transfixed to the spot.

A magnificent creature, the likes of which he had never seen, blocked the path.

It was three times his height, with a head like a horse, a body unlike anything he could ever imagine, and dragging behind the body, the tail of a crocodile!

The beast reared up on its hind legs, spread its great barbed wings, and snarled at the boy. "So, Arthur, you have dared return, but have no fear. You will never leave again!"

He tried to gather his thoughts. Just one step from a forest walk and now plunged into a strange land where fierce dragons talk. "My name is Matthew, not Arthur," was all he could get out — such was the fright he was in.

"Snivelling wretch," screamed the dragon, "would you deny your breeding in some vain effort to save your sorry skin? You disgust me. Yet, for all that, you will surely die."

In what seemed like a second, the beast had shackled the boy with a heavy iron band around his neck and was dragging him behind the snaking tail towards his castle.

"Have no fear wretch," the dragon called back to its captive, "dying in my dungeon you will — and have no concern for me. The stench of your rotting flesh will be as perfume to my fiendish nostrils."

Deep in the Dungeon

The beast was true to his word. The boy, now shackled deep in the castle dungeon, retched in the putrid stench. Bound in this dark, wet, vile place and, yes, absolutely out of his mind — as well as he may have been — with his reality snapped from one world into another. It was all too much to comprehend.

As his heart rate slowed and his eyes adjusted to the gloom, aided by a glimmer of light struggling through a crack in the wall, he called out.

"Hello, is anyone here?" He sought for some company in this dismal place with some fear should he find himself not alone.

"Here, beside you," came the voice of a young girl, "I am princess Bethany. The beast attacked our party, and has stolen me away, waiting for the ransom for my release. Were you sent to rescue me?"

"Ah, well, not exactly. I'm not from here, if you get my drift. I walked between a strange-looking tree and then, wow, I'm here in fantasy land, except the chains and the stench make it clear, this is no PlayStation game."

"PlayStation?"

"Forget it. You could not understand. I'm Matthew, nice to meet you, Bethany; I would, however, prefer another venue."

"Will your father; or anyone else, pay for your release Princess? Maybe they will let me go with you."

"I know of no-one in the king's service named Matthew. We had all hoped and prayed for the return of Arthur to restore peace and order."

"The dragon, or whatever it is, thought I was Arthur. Who is he?"

"A valiant knight who slew this dragon's father, but then disappeared; no one knows if he is alive or dead. The dragon, seeing the slain body of his father, has never rested. His mind was now deranged, his quest only to capture and kill Arthur."

"This doesn't sound all that promising to me Princess, looks like you and I have to escape, or die in this place. Let me see if I can reach you." Matthew stretched out his hand toward the voice. Clanking chains joined clanking chains, fingers to fingers, then hand to hand.

"Nice soft hands Bethany. Okay, we can reach each other. Now let me see what we can do about these locks."

"No-one has ever undone the dragon's locks, Matthew," the princess sighed.

"Well, here's the thing, my cousin Ralph is a reformed car thief and one summer he showed me some stuff. Let's see what we can do."

"What's a car, Matthew?"

"Later Princess. I'll explain if I can later. Now stretch out your hand."

Struggling to reach into the pocket of his jacket, Matthew drew out a paper clip, a good-luck charm from his cousin. "If I can get one hand free, then we are on our way Bethany." Trying to remember what Ralph told him, Matthew worked the paper clip into the lock clamped tight around Bethany's hand. Now dragon locks are super strong, but Matthew's paper clip was up to the task.

"I think I have it!" Matthew sighed, gently easing the Draconian tumblers this way and that and, with a final 'click,' the lock gave way.

"My hand is free!"

"Shush Bethany, we don't want any visitors, do we."

"Sorry, Matthew."

"Okay. Now, this may be a little tricky, but you have to pick the lock on my hand; I can't reach my other wrist."

Carefully, passing the paper clip to Bethany, Matthew, as best he could, tutored the king's daughter in the finer aspects of lock-picking.

"It's too hard, Matthew. I can't do it!"

"You have to, Bethany, or we both will rot in here. Not something I would care to do, and it would be a shame for the king's daughter to face the same end."

"Right, one more try, Bethany. Gently now, feel the tumblers in the lock moving, make like the paper clip is your gentle soft fingers, ease the tumblers over one another."

'Click.'

"Well done, Princess," Matthew whispered, "now hand me back the paper clip so I can undo the rest of the locks."

Matthew skilfully undid the last of the chains, but on hearing rumbling sounds from above, knew there was no time for formal introductions. Grasping Bethany's hand, they dashed up the steps and into the sunlight.

Bethany's Freedom

"You will never be safe here Princess, come with me," Matthew pleaded as they moved through the grounds towards the forked tree. She looked at the tree; the concept of another world, another time, was all too much for her. "Besides," she told him, "I am the king's daughter, and need to help lead the people here."

By now, the dragon had discovered their escape. Roaring like it would tear the sky, he rampaged through the castle looking for them until, standing high on a turret, he spied them making their way from the castle. His eyes glowing red with anger, he stormed after them.

"Run Bethany, run!" yelled Matthew. "I'll distract him so you can escape."

Quickly, the princess took off a necklace she had hidden from the dragon and pulled it over Matthew's head.

"Remember me." She squeezed his hands and fled into the dense woods.

Matthew's Escape

Unarmed, but now strangely unafraid, Matthew yelled at the dragon, "I may not be Arthur, but in time, I will destroy you, just as he dispatched your vile father!"

Incensed, the dragon focused solely on Matthew, determined to kill him outright.

Matthew ran through the woods faster than he thought possible. Too large to fit between the trees, the dragon crashed into some and tore down others in his chase, but all the while, Matthew was escaping.

Knowing that by now Bethany would have been safe, Matthew tried to make his way back to the forked tree, only to find the dragon waiting for him. The dragon was much weakened by the chase. His scales were bleeding, gashed by the broken branches. Then, striking a fearsome pose, the dragon raised himself high on his hind legs, screaming threats of destruction.

Just as the dragon lifted his head high once more to roar, Matthew, seeing his chance to escape, scrambled between the dragon's legs and reached the tree. Without looking back, Matthew squeezed between the tree limbs and pushed as hard as he could.

A new Knight in the Kingdom

Meanwhile, Bethany, tired and bruised, finally reached the safety of a nearby town. The villagers soon carried her to the castle and to her waiting father.

"Quickly," ordered the king, "get her inside; Maids, help her to her room to rest."

As she passed the king, though too exhausted to explain everything, she told her father, "An unknown knight rescued me, Father; he used strange words, but risked his life to save mine."

Later, after resting and having her wounds attended to, she sat with the king, trying to explain all that had happened. All the details of her capture; being locked in the dreadful dungeon, and the miraculous escape at the hands of her knight, Sir Matthew.

"Do you think he is safe, Bethany?" asked her father.

"Yes, he showed me what he said was a secret escape path through a forked tree. He wanted me to go with him, but I could not."

"Will he return my child?"

"That is my prayer. I gave him my token; the one mother gave me when I was born. That will draw him back."

Welcome Home

"What are you doing there?" His sister, standing over him, glared down.

Bruised and exhausted, he had fallen asleep in front of the tree.

"And why are your clothes so dirty and smelly? Where have you been?"

She seemed pleased to have found him, but had a twinge of anger at his state and recent disappearance.

"Not now, I'm bushed." Matthew struggled to reply. "Where's Dad?"

"I left him down at the stile, down near those large rocks. We had better get back to him fast."

As she helped him to his feet, she noticed the necklace, the rich gold chain and, at the base, a beautiful ruby.

"Where did you get this? Did you steal it?" she demanded.

"Someone gave it to me; leave it alone, sis. I'll explain what I can later. Now I just need a hot bath and a good sleep."

"You need a bath because you stink. Well, where have you been?"

Bethany to the Rescue

The trouble with Bling

"You need to stop wearing that necklace, it just isn't right!" Matthew's sister snapped at him.

Matthew had worn the necklace every day after coming back from his adventure. His sister had a point, though. There weren't many boys in Wales who had a heavy gold necklace with a massive ruby on the end, let alone any who wore it every day. Wearing it brought back memories of Bethany and the dragon; how could he forget the dragon? After about a week, he put the necklace in his top drawer, deciding it might be better not to wear it. He looked at it every day, though.

It must have been about 2 o'clock in the morning when he woke with a start. A strange glow filled the room that seemed to come from his top drawer. A little anxious, he got out of bed and opened the drawer. There, right in front, was the necklace, the ruby now not just a deep red, it glowed like a lamp!

Reaching in, he picked up the gold chain and pulled it over his head, tucking the ruby inside his pyjama top as he went back to bed. Strange dreams and feelings came into his mind. He felt such a pain and a longing to be somewhere—somewhere else.

I have to get help

Meanwhile, back in the land behind the forked tree, the dragon, robbed of his prisoners by the impudent youth who had crept into his land, was angrier than he had ever been. Daily he left his castle and roamed the countryside looking for the princess and the strange boy who called himself Matthew. He came to the farmers, demanding to know where they were. If the farmer couldn't say, the dragon would burn down the farmer's cottage and set his crops on fire. The terrible news soon reached the King's ears, but he was now too old to fight a dragon.

Princess Bethany, though afraid of being captured by the dragon once more, knew something or someone had to stop the dragon before it destroyed all the kingdom, so went to talk to her father. "Father, I must find my knight; he is the only one I know who can help us."

"My child, you are too precious for me to allow you to risk your life this way," and so forbade the princess to leave the castle.

Day by day the dragon kept destroying more farms, leaving less and less food for the people to eat.

Bethany went again to the king, "Father, I am the only one who can find the tree that leads to the world where Matthew lives. Let me try to find him. Our situation is desperate."

Bethany goes to the future

After a night of pacing and worry, the old king agreed. Bethany disguised herself in boy's clothing so the dragon, should he find her walking alone, would not realise who she was. Knowing the dragon slept in the late afternoon, she planned to escape to the other world just before dark.

Walking past the shuttered cottages of the town's folk, all hiding, afraid of the dragon's temper, and through the burned-out fields, keeping a watch out for any noise or sight, she made her way through the forbidding forest in the fading light.

Afraid it would be dark before she could find the tree and trapped in the dragon's estate, she ran through the trees, falling several times. Many broken branches littered the forest floor, an obvious reminder of the frantic chase the dragon made trying to re-capture Matthew when they had escaped from the dungeon.

The last rays of the sun crept over the western hills when she came to where the forked tree grew. Holding onto the trunks, she looked around. A wave of fear came over her. She could see nothing through the limbs except more trees. She had refused to go with Matthew when they had escaped. Now she had to go alone, alone into a strange world, not even knowing where to search for her knight. With a deep sigh, she pushed through the thick limbs into Matthew's world.

Darkness descended. Afraid, Bethany stayed by the tree all night. Strange sounds came to her ears. Strange lights moved about in what she thought must be a valley lower down from the tree where she crouched.

At first light, she left the tree and made her way down the hill, following a clear path through the trees and small streams that flowed down into the valley. The noises she heard during the night became louder as she neared the valley floor. The path had signs with words, but she could not understand their meaning.

Monsters Everywhere

Approaching a clearing, a roaring sound bellowed. Terrified it could be another dragon, she hid behind a tree. Soon, a mechanical monster loomed through the trees. In the morning light, she could make out many wheels and what seemed to be a man riding the beast along a black track that swept through the valley. The monster disappeared as soon as it had appeared. She realised it cannot have been looking for her and came from behind the tree, walking across the clearing to where a small building stood near the black track. Looking up, she spied long lines in the sky reaching from one dead tree to another.

"What have I done?" she slumped to the ground, terrified by the monsters that seemed to appear out of nowhere then vanish just as fast. Entering the building, she hoped to find someone to ask directions from, but there was no sign of life. Pictures lined the walls. Some seemed familiar to her, like castles and forts, but nothing that would help her find her knight.

Peering from the safety of the building, Bethany watched. As each monster passed, her fear of being attacked subsided. Sometimes she could see a whole family inside the mechanical beast; they all seemed happy or just looked around at things as they passed by.

Across the black track, she could see a small river running down through the valley. In her land, a similar stream started high in the mountains and flowed down past the castle and into the town. Thinking Matthew might live in a town downstream, she decided walking along the bank of the river would be the best way to find him. Afraid, she left the building and walked across the hard black surface the mechanical beasts rode on, but after only a few steps, another mechanical machine swept around the bend and, with a fearful blast from what she thought was its mouth, headed straight towards her.

In terror, she fled to the side of the track nearest the water to escape. The monster roared again as it sped past, missing her by inches. With only a few trees between the water and the monster's track, she hid, sobbing out of control.

Together again

Meanwhile, Matthew planned to fish upstream from the town. After breakfast, he rode out from Beddgelert toward Dinas Emrys. Coming to the carpark next to the walking tracks, his thoughts returned to the forked tree. The ruby necklace throbbed, or so it felt to him. It was then he heard crying coming from the bank of the river.

With his mind distracted by the sound of what seemed to be that of a girl, he stopped to investigate. Parking his bike against a tree, he walked to the bank of the stream. There, huddled over and sobbing, was what seemed to be a boy, but the voice was much higher pitched. By now, the Ruby was almost jumping up and down inside his shirt.

"Hello, are you all right? What's the matter?" he called out.

The weeping slowed; the stranger turned to look where the voice had come from. With her hair tucked up inside the cap, Matthew could not recognise Bethany, and she, now trying to wipe away the tears with her sleeve, and still in great fear, could not recognise her knight.

"The monster frightened me, and I didn't know what to do." Bethany's words came out all jumbled, and she cried again.

"Monster, what monster?" Matthew walked closer to the stranger.

"The one that chased me on the black track, it roared at me!"

Just then, a truck came into view. Bethany froze in fear. "There is another one; oh help me, please!"

"It's just a truck on the road. It can't hurt you." Matthew looked at the boy. "Who are you? What's your name and how did you get here with no bike or car?"

Bethany was not keen to let anyone know who she was. "I just walked here from up on the hill."

"How far up the hill?" Matthew's interest intensified. Could it be someone who had come through the tree just as he had? That would explain the strange conversation about trucks and cars. Sitting down beside the boy; not too close, maybe a foot or so away. He waited for a response. The Ruby was glowing bright and throbbing like the beating of his heart.

"I don't want to say," came the reply, but as she spoke, the glow of the ruby shone through Matthew's shirt. "What is glowing on your chest?" she asked and stared at her new companion.

"It's just a gift I had from a friend," Matthew, now also a little coy, replied.

Bethany's eyes widened. She tried to wipe away the tears so she could see. "Show me, please. It's important!" Her pleading voice weakening his resolve.

"Okay, just don't laugh, all right?" and, undoing the top buttons, he pulled the necklace out. The ruby glowed bright red.

"Matthew, Matthew!" Bethany screamed and hugged him. "I have come looking for you!" Her cap fell off and her beautiful long hair flowed over her shoulders.

"Bethany?"

"Yes, yes, it's me!"

Go Back?

"What are you doing here? It is so dangerous for you to be here. This is a very different place than what you are used to."

"The dragon is killing people and burning the crops trying to find you. The kingdom is being destroyed. Please, you need to come back with me to help!"

Matthew slumped; the first time had been an accident. They were both lucky to have escaped with their lives; but now, to return and fight the dragon, well, that was a whole other matter.

"Matthew, you saved me. You are my knight. Now you have to save the entire kingdom. This is your quest!" Bethany held him close and, face to face, kissed him.

"Oh brother," Matthew gasped, first from the shock of being kissed by a princess, and second from the realisation that what she had said was true. He had to go back.

"When did you last eat, Bethany?"

"Yesterday, before I left the castle."

"OK, let's see what mum packed for me," and with that he drew out the lunch box from his knapsack. Inside were two sandwiches, an apple, and an orange.

"Looks like ham and tomato; how does that sound to you?"

Bethany screwed her nose up at the thought.

"Ok, you eat the fruit, and I'll eat the sandwiches; they are nice, you know, fit even for a princess." He smiled and handed her the apple. Matthew was thinking about what to do next. He couldn't take Bethany home with him, too many questions, but they couldn't stay on the bank of the river either. Bethany looked at Matthew, sensing his concerns.

"We have to go back now Matthew, the dragon sleeps in the afternoon and if we don't get back to the castle tonight, I don't know what will happen."

Matthew sighed, "Okay, I guess you are right. I'll just have to leave a note on my bike; they will freak out, but it's better than nothing. Let's see what I have here in the fishing bag that might be of use to us." Tipping all the contents out onto the ground, he took the knife and some heavy sinkers of lead, unsure why, but maybe the story of David and Goliath had something to do with it. Scribbling a note, he tied it to the handlebars with a fishing line.

Bethany paced up and down, eager to be on her way.

"Settle down Bethany, all right? We will be at the tree in just over an hour, plenty of time to get you home before dark." Taking her hand, they crossed the road and started the climb up to the track leading to the old hill fort.

"What are these signs Matthew, I can't read them?"

"These tracks lead to an old hill fort made by old King Vortigern. He had some issues with some dragons just like you do, but Merlin stepped in and sorted it all out. Have you heard of Merlin?"

"No, and we don't have time for a history lesson. I can keep up."

"Yes, my Princess," Matthew bowed, and, taking her hand, led the way over the styles, around the hill, by the pool with the waterfall, and came to the forked tree, ominous and brooding, standing in the way.

Bethany caught around Matthew and kissed him. "I can't do this in my country, so you will just have to remember how it was."

The afternoon sun was low, shadows crept across the valley floor as they approached the tree.

"Let me go first. If everything is okay, I'll pull you through." Matthew, now playing the knight, squeezed through into the other world. Looking and listening, he waited. Sensing no evidence of the dragon's presence, pulled his princess through the tree and back into her own world.

"Glad to be back?" he asked with a smile.

"Yes, your world is as frightening to me as I suppose mine was to you, and perhaps still is."

"Ok, let's get you home and work out what we have to do."

Back up to the tree

Within an hour, the young pair entered a local village. Smoke was still rising from a burned field—the dragon hadn't taken a day off. It was not long before they arrived at the castle where her father, anxious to see his daughtter again, waited.

"This is Sir Matthew?" The king, incredulous, asked as they entered the castle.

"Yes, father, but he brings knowledge of things unknown to us from another time. The things I saw today were amazing, and impossible to describe; he will use his world's knowledge to defeat the dragon."

"Is it true, my son, can you actually do all what my daughter has just told me?"

"Well Sir, my world is more advanced than yours, though I would not say it is any better; we have got rid of all the dragons, so that says something!"

"Well, most welcome you are, my son, for we are in dire straights, and without a deliverer, we will surely perish at the hand of the dragon."

The king organised a room for Matthew in the castle. Over dinner, they discussed what they might do.

What's been going on?

Next day, not long after sunrise, they could hear the dreadful roar of the dragon nearing the town. Matthew ran to the top of the castle to see what would happen. Even though the dragon's fire had burned most of the fields, the beast still roamed the town, screaming demands for the whereabouts of Matthew and Arthur. Then, enraged, Matthew saw him set fire to the thatched roof of a cottage, forcing the family to flee for their lives. Bethany joined Matthew on the battlements to witness the proceedings, though, being careful not to be seen from the town below. "Your dragon doesn't seem to fly," Matthew commented. "That could help us."

"Yes, but he is still very large, fierce and breathes fire," Bethany reminded him.

"True, my Princess, but he is also cumbersome to the point of clumsiness. I think we could use that weakness. Let me think more about how we could exploit this."

"Please; but not too long, my brave knight." Bethany looked longingly into his eyes.

As they looked over the town, the dragon turned and, roaring all the time, returned through the woods to his castle.

"He seems to follow the same path to and from his castle, Bethany, we could build a trap for him on that path."

The king and Matthew discussed the plan all morning, agreeing it was the only way, though it would put the young knight's life in peril.

Checking out the Dragon

"There has to be another way!" Bethany complained when told of the scheme; her affection for Matthew growing to where her father might become suspicious of the relationship.

"Do you have any rubber, Bethany?"

"I don't know what rubber is, Matthew!" Bethany sighed.

"Never mind, I will have to make a slingshot instead," he muttered as he walked to the workshop deep inside the castle.

The king arranged for all the town's leaders, in secret, to come to the castle where he explained Matthew's plan to them all. With their lives in the balance, all were keen to assist. Throughout the day, the men of the town prepared for the evening's toil; no digging could start until the dragon was asleep.

At the risk of being seen, Matthew and Bethany walked to the woods, noting precisely the way the dragon went to and from the town through the trees. "Here, here is the spot!" Matthew exclaimed as they came to a bend in the path. He marked out the area so the men would know where to prepare that night.

Late in the afternoon, dozens of energetic men gathered in the woods. Matthew explained the plan again, then the work began. Late into the night, they toiled to complete Matthew's plan; then, exhausted, they returned to their homes, hoping the plan would work.

Bethany fretted all night. It was to be a substantial risk Matthew would take in the morning. Matthew, however, seemed unconcerned as he completed his weapon.

"What are you going to do?" Bethany asked.

"I need to make the dragon so mad at me he will not be thinking straight, and then, while he is chasing me, we will trap him. Well, that's the plan," he tried to smile to cheer her up.

The plan hatched

Before the sun rose the next day, Matthew crept through the town and to the path leading towards the dragon's castle, but not so near as the dragon might catch him before they could spring the trap.

Very few slept in the town or castle that night; what would unfold in the first light of day would determine their fate, and that of their young knight, the lad, from another time and place.

The dragon's mind, though deranged, had only one thought: the death of this Matthew, who had taunted him and escaped. In keeping with his pattern, the dragon, awakened by the sunrise, renewed in his crazed determination to find the young knight, stormed from his castle and headed for the town. As he approached the woods that marked the boundary of his land and that of the king, a slim figure emerged from the shadows.

"Halt vile fiend, you will go no further!" Matthew screamed at the dragon.

Stunned by the effrontery of the boy, the dragon stopped, looked down, and sneered.

"Are you such a fool, boy, that you think you can elude me twice? You shall be my breakfast; here will I shed your blood!" Rearing up on his hind legs, the dragon roared at the young knight who, like another young man so many years before, swung the leather strap loaded with the lead fishing weight around his head. Then, releasing the sinker, watched it fly straight into the left eye of the dragon, blinding him.

The dragon screamed in pain and anger.

Matthew dashed towards the trees.

Seeing with only one eye, the dragon gave chase, crashing into trees, breathing fire with every stride.

Baiting the Trap

Matthew was only some twenty paces in front of the rampaging beast. "Only a hundred yards to go!" he breathed to himself as the fire from the dragon's nostrils licked at the branches close to his racing feet. "I sure hope this works!" Matthew prayed as he rounded the bend leading to the trap. Looking to the side, he spied the rope dangling from a tree; at full speed, he launched himself onto the rope and flew over the trap.

The dragon, incensed, injured and out of his mind, careered around the bend in the woods, the death of the young upstart his only goal.

Slipping as he went around the corner, he failed to see the false covering on the path and, with a hellish shriek, fell into the pit the villagers had dug the night before. Sharpened spikes, as tall as a man, drove into the dragon as he fell. Fire and blood, screams and curses rent the morning air.

Matthew crept to the edge of the pit. There, trapped, the dragon lay impaled on the spikes. Now that the hideous screams of the dragon had ceased, the townsfolk, in trepidation, crept through the woods to where they had set the trap. There they found Matthew, staring down onto the writhing form of the dragon.

Cheering erupted as the townsfolk carried Matthew back to the castle in triumph. Waiting at the drawbridge, Bethany and the king cheered as they saw Matthew approaching with the crowd from the village.

Bethany rushed forward to meet her knight, and, forgetting royal protocol, hugged and kissed her champion. The king, elated at the defeat of the dragon, forgot to chastise his daughter's emotional outburst.

The kiss between the young dragon slayer and the princess did not go unnoticed by the townsfolk, who cheered again as the young couple embraced.

Matthew stopped, "It's not yet done," he realised, "I need a stake and a hammer!" Grasping them from a nearby farmer, he raced back through the town, returning to the where the dragon lay. All the townsfolk followed and waited at the lip of the pit as Matthew climbed down onto the impaled beast.

Critically wounded, the dragon was still alive, as, unlike other creatures, it could not be dispatched so easily. The Dragon struggled against the spikes and tried to bite Matthew as he lowered himself onto its chest. Smoke and fumes still came from the dragon's mouth as Matthew raised the stake over the heart of the monster.

Screaming, the dragon begged Matthew not to kill him, promising never to harm the town again. But with one last shriek, he died as Matthew hammered the spike into its heart.

"Fill the pit," yelled the knight as he climbed back over the bank. "Let not one ounce of air enter to where the beast lies."

Hundreds of townsfolk shovelled and stamped over the dead dragon. Hour after hour, they shovelled and stamped and cheered.

A problem with the king

Exhausted, Matthew and Bethany walked back to the castle, hand in hand.

"What now, my knight?" Bethany looked into his eyes.

"Sleep, my Princess, sleep."

"No, what now!" she squeezed his hand.

"Later, here comes your father."

"Matthew, Matthew my son, well done; you have saved us. What will you have?"

Bethany nudged Matthew in the ribs.

"Ah, well, if it would please your majesty, Bethany and I, well, see, we kind of like each other, and so, if you could see your way clear to allow us to, you know, get married, that would be okay with me. There is a catch, though. My folks know nothing about here, about you or Bethany or the dragon; there will be some explaining to do, do you understand?"

"Do you mean you want to go back? Why?"

"Well, it gets worse I'm afraid, I need to ask you to let Bethany come back with me for a while, just a little while, so she can see my world, meet my parents, and my sister, and then we will come back. How does that sound?"

"I don't like the way it sounds at all, young man. I don't care what magnificent feats you have done today; I will never let Bethany leave the kingdom again. Do you hear me?"

"Ah, yes sir, I think you have made your point very clear."

"Bother," he thought, "What a mess I'm in now."

"I tell you what, your highness, I'll show you on a map where I live so that if anyone comes looking for me after I go through the tree, you can find me. I'm thrilled that we have taken care of the dragon, but if you will not allow Bethany to come with me, then I will have to go alone."

Matthew lifted off the necklace and handed it back to Bethany. "I wish you well, my Princess," and kissed her.

"No, Matthew, no," screamed Bethany, "you can't go!"

"This is something you will have to work out with your father; I have to go."

Turning his back on the king and his daughter, Matthew walked through the cheering crowd and back to the tree.

Not going so well

"Where is your gold necklace?" his sister demanded.

"Gave it back," was all he could say.

"Where have you been, Matthew? The note said you would be gone for a little while, like hours, not days!" yelled his father.

"Sorry Dad, just something I had to take care of; all sorted now."

A Knight in Fright

"Where is your brother? His dinner will go cold?" Matthew's mother demanded.

"Probably sulking in his room; he's been like that ever since he came back after leaving his bike by the river and disappearing for days," his sister commented.

"Matthew," his father called out, "your dinner is going cold."

"Leave him Dad, it will serve him right if it goes cold." His sister was still fuming that Matthew hadn't told her where he had been on his last adventure.

With a crash the outside door flew open, and what seemed straight out of Disneyland, a medieval knight, old and beaten-up, lurched into the room, stumbled over the doorstep and almost fell headfirst onto the table just missing a bowl of potatoes. Trying to regain his composure, the old knight struggled to his feet. "I call Sir Matthew to his destiny!"

"His what?" his sister blurted out.

"Who are you, wench, to question a king's knight? You will keep silent when I speak. I command you to deliver Sir Matthew immediately!" With that, the old man drew his sword, brandishing it in the air, just missing the kitchen light. As the meal descended into confusion, Matthew entered; his father's angry tone plus his own hunger roused him from the anguish he had felt since leaving Bethany.

The two standing figures looked at each other across the room. "Matthew?" the old knight asked.

"Arthur?" Matthew questioned.

"The saints be praised. I have found you. We must return forthwith or the kingdom will collapse." Arthur's voice was full of urgency.

Matthew noticed the drawn sword. "Put up your sword Arthur, there is no danger here. Besides, it is dark and there is no way we could find the tree tonight. Please try to relax. You seem totally spent. Did you walk all the way here from the hill?"

Slowly, the old man relaxed, slipping the gleaming sword back into the scabbard as he slumped into a chair by the fire.

Dinner with friends

In shock, the family said not a word. Well, not since Matthew's sister's outburst, anyway. The three stunned faces looked at Arthur, then at Matthew, then back to the old knight.

"Well," Matthew began, "I'll try to explain as best I can later, but Mum, while I try to get Arthur out of his armour, would you get him something to eat, please?" Matthew walked to where Arthur sat motionless and tried to unbuckle the sword and then take off his mud-covered boots.

"Matthew," the old knight stopped him, "should not the wench perform this task?"

"Arthur," Matthew tried not to laugh, "the wench is my sister. The world you are in is a little different from the one you are comfortable with; I don't mind helping and I have a thousand questions to ask, but perhaps not right now."

Matthew gazed into the old man's face; the exposure to cars and trucks and other frights he would have faced had taken a toll on the knight's stamina and comprehension.

Arthur just nodded, allowing him to remove the heavy outer layer of clothing.

The rest of the family looked on in wonder. Matthew's sister, with eyes of fire following the 'wench' title, surveyed the man from out of time who now sat in their kitchen.

Gender Issues

A little later, Arthur, now able to move about, took in his surroundings; the family seated around the table was easy, their clothing odd to his understanding but not so far removed from his own wardrobe.

"It might be easier if you sat at the table, Arthur," Matthew suggested. Making room, the family and their guest sat together.

Arthur, tired but hungry, soon finished the meat and vegetables Matthew's mother had dished up.

"Would you care for a beer, Arthur?" Matthew's father attempted a conversation with the knight.

Arthur lifted his gaze from the plate to where the voice came from. "My host, I would most appreciate a draught of ale; my journey here today has taken its toll on my stamina and nerves; never in my life have I been so hard pressed to carry on. Mechanical beasts charged me at every turn; I would face a dozen dragons in preference."

"So, Arthur," Matthew's sister chipped in, "have you actually seen a live dragon?"

"In deference to your brother and my host, I will speak to you, however you will address me as Sir Arthur. I am a knight of the realm and though, as I am informed, you are no wench, your manners belie their recommendation. Yes, I have both seen, fought and killed dragons. Does that answer your question?"

Matthew's sister, now put into her place by the old knight, replied, "Thank you, Sir Arthur, you are the bravest person I have ever met."

"Your brother," Arthur replied, "is a most brave dragon slayer. I have heard reports that, at the risk of his life, first led one through a forest and at another time climbed down a pit to drive a stake through a beast's heart, saving an entire kingdom."

"Matthew," his mother in shock looked at her son, "you mentioned none of this."

Matthew shrugged his shoulders, "It was all in another time and place, Mum. Besides, it would have just freaked you out."

Wide eyed, his sister looked at him. "You have killed a dragon?"

"Yes, but I had a bit of help." Matthew's modesty becoming that of a knight.

Questions

The beer soon took its toll on the old knight; his head nodded towards the table. Mathew's mother caught the fall before he hurt himself.

"I'll take Arthur to sleep in my bed, Mum. Dad, would you give me a hand, please?" The two eased the tired old man from the table and up to Matthew's bed; a mumbled thanks from the knight bidding them all good evening.

Back in the kitchen, all eyes were on Matthew. "What on earth has been going on, son?" his father asked on behalf of them all.

"I had only heard of Arthur, Dad; seems he killed the first dragon then disappeared. My stumbling through the forked tree ended with me having to fight that dragon's son—he was not a jovial chap, to be sure. As far as I can see, Arthur has returned from wherever he went, seen that the land was not in a happy state and has come to fetch me back."

"Are you really a knight?" his sister stared at him.

"Well, yes, I guess so Sis. Things are different there. I had to do some stuff to help and, well, basically I am now meant to marry the king's daughter."

"How can you get married? You are only sixteen!" screamed his mother?

"Sorry, Mum, but that's the way it is. The fact I sort of saved the land meant I had to marry the princess; she is rather cute though. I tried to get her to come and meet you all but as the king refused, I had to come back alone, never really planning to go back. Arthur has changed all that."

"If you go back with Arthur now, son, what then?" his father asked, staring at a son he only thought he knew.

"Ah, if I go back, I will never return; that's just the way it will have to be. There Dad I am needed; stuff happened and the son you know, is not the same person once I pass through the tree's forks. The strain on everyone will be too great to transition through time again. I know it is hard to get your head around it, but there really is a time warp or whatever you want to call it, and though I don't know why. I'm meant to be there. Sorry."

"Can I visit?" his sister asked.

"I'm not sure sis, I sort of doubt it though. People have walked through the tree trunks for years and nothing ever happened; why it works for me, I do not understand. Look, it will probably be a long day tomorrow. I'll sleep on the couch if that's okay. Arthur might wake up in the night. If I don't, Dad, would you mind showing him the bathroom, please?" Matthew smiled, walked over, and hugged his mother. "I'll be fine Mum, don't worry."

"Will you need breakfast, dear?" she asked.

"That would be nice, Mum; it might take a while to get Arthur organised, anyway; hopefully Dad will take us out to the tourist centre so we don't attract undue attention." Everyone smiled. It would not be a goodnight; it was to be goodbye.

"What is her name, dear?" his mother asked, holding her son tight. "Bethany, Mum, Princess Bethany; you'd like her."

Arthur meets the Beast

It was a little difficult getting Arthur under the shower in the morning, but all the family knew that was what he needed to do.

Breakfast was a quiet affair; lots of long looks around the table. No one would or could have ever imagined a morning like this.

Arthur, eager to return, in part keen to leave this strange and forbidding place, paced around the room.

"Leave the sword off, Arthur," Matthew's father asked. "You will never get into the car with that on."

"Car?" Arthur replied.

"You will see one soon," Matthew comforted the old knight. "It will all be fine, just a little different, okay?"

"Different is not a word I would have ever used to describe what I have both heard and seen over this last day Matthew, indeed words completely fail me; my poor mind has been in turmoil since entering your world and I fear will remain in that state until I can return to mine." The old knight looked at Matthew. They both smiled at their shared experiences in strange worlds.

"May I carry your sword, Sir knight?" Matthew's sister respectfully approached Arthur. He looked at her, and realising the change in her attitude, handed her the sword. "Mind you take care of it, girl."

The family and their guest walked out of the front door into the morning light.

Arthur gasped, "There's one there, a mechanical beast!"

"That's a car, Arthur," Matthew's father tried to explain. "It is just a closed carriage, but no horses. The power comes from an engine in the

front; come and let me show you there is nothing to be concerned about."
The two walked towards the car. Matthew went to join them when his
mother called him back.

Leaving Home

"What is it Mum? We have to leave."

"I want you to take this with you, dear." She reached into her pocket
and drew out a small box. "It is my mother's wedding ring. Perhaps your
princess would like to have it as hers." Diamonds and rubies shone in the
sunlight.

"Thanks Mum, it is just beautiful. Bethany will be proud to wear it,
I'm sure." Matthew took the ring and hugged his mother tight.

"Matthew!" Arthur called with an anxious tone.

"Coming."

Still hesitant, Arthur slid into the back seat of the car, Matthew
climbed in on the other side.

"Your sword, Sir Arthur," Matthew's sister carefully slid the sheathed
weapon into the back seat of the car.

"Thank you, my child. May you live long and bear many sons." Arthur
smiled at her.

"I guess you are not a wench anymore, sis," Matthew grinned at her.
"Come and see us some time, through the forked tree and turn right. You
can't miss it."

Arthur jumped as the car moved off, his eyes wide in apprehension if
not outright fear.

Standing in the doorway, the two women waved as the car moved out
of the driveway and onto the road out of town. Only one occupant would
return.

"I hope we are there before the tourists, Dad," Matthew said. "Might
be a little awkward with Arthur climbing the hill along with school girls
with backpacks and walking sticks."

Arthur looked at him, "I Thought only old men used a walking stick, Matthew?"

Matthew and his father laughed. "These days, folk who go climbing around these hills have modern walking sticks to make it easier for them; I think sometimes it is just another way of getting money from gullible folk, Arthur."

Back to the tree

It wasn't long before they pulled into the car park at the foot of the climb to the old hill fort.

"Doesn't seem too busy, Matt, you should have a clear path to the tree."

The three climbed out of the car and shook hands.

"It was a pleasure to meet you, Arthur, and have you spend the evening with us. If I could ask you one thing, please watch over my son."

"Thank you, my host, for your vittles and lodging. Have no fear for Matthew, even though your son is an accomplished knight. As long as I am able, I will make sure he is safe."

Matthew hugged his father, "Not sure if I will ever be back, Dad, thank you for being my father. Please let mum know I will be fine…. love you."

"We need to go, Matthew." Arthur looked at the sky, the sun rising higher over the valley.

With a wave to his father, Matthew joined the old knight, who had already started the trek up the hill. Settling into a steady gait, the two climbed higher. Over styles, open fields, crossing streams with tiny slate bridges, they worked their way up to the tree.

The Quest

"So Arthur," Matthew began, "where did you go after you killed the first dragon? Everyone thought you had disappeared?"

"The Crusades Matthew, I went to fight the Moors in the Holy Land. A hard and bitter time, let me tell you. They also imprisoned me for a period, something I would rather not have to endure again. In the end, we were driven out of Jerusalem, so I just worked my way back here."

"But I thought you were a knight of the king?"

"There are many kings, young man, and many knights. I was never a knight to this king. As I travelled through the land, I helped where I could but never settled. Therefore, I returned to protect and help the kingdom here. I conversed with the princess on my return and this is how I learned of your unfortunate departure, that, and what else I perceived in the land, drove me to fetch you back."

"Probably just as well. I was not in a happy place after I returned. What do you think about this time-shift thing?"

"Do you mean what happens when we pass through the tree? In all my life, I have never heard or seen the like. It has to be about you, just you, Matthew."

"But you have travelled through the tree, Bethany, also, so it cannot be just about me. Perhaps it is about the three of us."

"These are dark thoughts, my young knight. My old mind is tired enough. Let us go to the tree and there to do what needs doing once through the boughs."

"As you wish." Matthew, sensing the old man's weariness, ceased the discussion.

Rounding the last bend, they clambered over the moss-covered rock outcrops. There, before them, stood the tree.

As they approached, Arthur turned to his young apprentice. "This may well be your last passage. Are you resolved to do what needs to be done?"

"I wasn't until we scaled the hill together. Now I am convinced this is my lot, my quest. Is this how I should feel?"

"This way and no other. There must be no shred of double-mindedness, there must only be the quest."

Matthew shivered. The nearer they came to the tree, a coldness descended upon him, not fear, but foreboding.

"Now Matthew, delay not!" The old knight urged.

With one hand on the old knight and the other on the main trunk, Matthew drew himself and Arthur after him back into the world of kings, dragons, and Bethany.

A moments Hesitation

A warm, soft afternoon breeze greeted the two knights. There was no sign of the events about to unfold.

"Let us to the castle, Matthew; the king, and no doubt the lovely Bethany, will be most pleased to see you."

As they passed through the farms, labourers toiling waved from every field.

"No doubt news of your return, my young friend, will soon run through the land like a summer grass fire." Arthur smiled and patted Mathew's shoulder.

As they neared the town, a small crowd had already gathered to welcome them; the citizens, now safe from the ravages of the dragon and, remembering the young knight's exploits, all hoped for a brighter future.

Matthew, however, was unsure as to his reception in the castle after leaving as he had. Would the abrupt departure have caused concerns over his loyalty and affection for the young princess? Feeling in his pocket for the tiny metal case containing his grandmother's wedding ring, he hoped for reassurance.

The band of villagers accompanied the two knights as they approached the castle. At the bridge over the moat, the townsfolk stopped, leaving Matthew and Arthur to cross alone.

Arthur, pleased to be once more in familiar surroundings, strode forward, as best an old knight can. Matthew, with a more hesitant step, fell somewhat behind.

"Come, my friend, mend your gait. This is a merry homecoming!" Arthur called back, aware of his friend's apprehension.

All is forgiven

With some twenty paces before they would reach the doors, they paused. Heavy beams opened to reveal the waiting king and princess just inside the walls. On his strict instructions Bethany, impatient, stood at his side, forced to wait for her beloved to enter the castle. Her wide smile and sparking eyes welcoming, Matthew gave a sigh of relief. His own face now reflected hers; all would be well.

Taking a lead from his mentor, Matthew lowered his head in respect to the king, who stepped forward to grasp first Arthur's, then Matthew's hands.

"It does my old heart glad to see you both returned, and you, young man, I trust your presence with us will not be so casually dismissed as your last." Matthew blushed red. Bethany reached out and took Matthew's hand, squeezing hard.

"Come, let us inside. There is much to discuss," the king commanded. Arthur, at the king's side, Bethany and Matthew fell behind, looking into each other's eyes as they all made their way into the castle.

A Plan rejected

The threat

After dinner, they dispensed with formalities. As the huge log fire crackled at the end of the room, the king recounted reports from his spies of an impending invasion. "There have been disputes over certain parcels of lands for generations. We have managed by diplomatic means to keep the peace. However, the new king of Powys, with an eye to public popularity, as a diversion from his ineptitude, has however determined by force to claim dominion of several towns and villages under our rule."

"Have you attempted dialogue, your highness?" Arthur asked.

"Many times. I have sent messengers to his court craving discussions, but they have rejected all out of hand; the last emissary narrowly escaped with his life."

"Can he raise a large force, sir?" Matthew asked.

"Our information is that he is attempting to build an army of ten thousand, some regular soldiers, but it seems he is bent on conscripting many civilians to swell the ranks."

"What will you do, Father?" Bethany asked, drawing near to the king.

"We are in difficult straits, my child. I would, of course, defend our land, but as we have lived in peace for so long, we have had no need of an army, so apart from a small guard, we have no soldiers to speak of. My fear is," the king continued, "that should we not contest this incursion, it will only embolden him to push further and further into our lands; it is a significant problem."

Lovers reunited

Though concerned with the welfare of the country, Matthew and Bethany slipped away from the firelight to embrace high on the battlements.

"My heart died when you left me standing there; you must have known I could never disobey my father."

"It was a difficult time, having little to do with love. Love was never a question. It was a test, perhaps for both of us." He held her close and kissed her.

"What will you do? You must save us," she pleaded.

"Luck, bravado, and a paper clip will not save us now, my princess. We must think of a plan; I need to speak with Arthur."

The Almanac

Entering the study, they found the king and the old knight deep in conversation. Digging into his coat pocket, Matthew drew out a Welsh almanac. "My sister must have put this in here," he thought. Sitting by the fireside, he leafed through the pages until a wild thought crossed his mind.

"Arthur, what year is it? Month and day, quickly; I need to know." Matthew broke into the discussion.

"What ails you, my son?" the king asked.

"Well, sir, this book tells of all the great and interesting things that have happened in Welsh history and I am hoping we could match up what we are going through now to what may be of use to us soon."

"I am sorry my son, I don't understand," the king shook his head.

"It is November the sixth in the year of our Lord Twelve Hundred and Thirteen, but why the concern, Matthew?" Arthur responded.

Matthew didn't answer. He leafed through the book, trying to find the year and date. Maybe, just maybe, something happened that could be of use in the kingdom's defence.

More Questions

"What is the name of your kingdom, your highness?" Matthew asked, his head still buried in the pages.

"Why Gwynedd, of course. Why would you have not known that?"

"Well, I'm sorry to have to tell you, sir, it's all just called Wales now, no more kingdoms."

The king looked at Matthew. "And what of Powys? Is that also gone?"

"Yes, my king, there are no small kingdoms left." It concerned Matthew the king might just give up now, knowing all the Welsh kings had ceased to be. "Is Powys your enemy, sir?"

"Yes, Matthew, he is the one troubling our land."

"Do you think he will attack soon?" Matthew questioned the king.

"He would not launch an attack with winter approaching. I suspect he will wait until March or April of next year. We should be able to develop a small force by then."

"So that would be Twelve Hundred and Fourteen," Matthew muttered to himself and continued to search for the date. "Wow," he exclaimed, "they never told me this in the history class, or maybe I was just not paying attention. Anyway, it says here that early in Twelve Hundred and Fourteen there was a massive earthquake in this valley in eastern mid-Wales. There is even a picture of the valley. Do you know this place?" Matthew handed the book to the king. Arthur looked over the king's shoulder to see. "I know this place Matthew," Arthur announced, "and also, I believe this would be the path the king of Powys must take in his attempt to seize the estates."

"What are you saying happened?" The king looked in amazement at the young knight?

"Now, this is all out there, you understand, but with all that has happened, I'll believe almost anything is possible. If we can lure your foe into the valley at the exact time, there will be the possibility, a very slim one I admit, an earthquake will destroy both him and his army, or if not, at least disrupt them by the tremors which would occur before and after."

The King is unsure

"What is an earthquake, Matthew?" Arthur, now agitated by Matthew's ramblings.

"Ok, I won't go into all the details, but sometimes the earth moves as a lot of pressure builds up under the surface. Like if you bend a branch, it will only bend so far before it snaps. The earth behaves the same way. Often vast gaps occur, causing significant damage until it all settles down again. Does that make any sense?"

"Are you telling me your plan is that the earth will swallow up my enemy?" the king was incredulous.

"Yes, I'm afraid that is it. We have to lure him, so he stays in the valley for as long as possible, as I don't know the exact date of the earthquake. Even if his army is not destroyed, fear should do the rest and those remaining will all head back home."

"This plan is utter madness, young man. Only a fool would consider such a thing. Because of your previous service to my kingdom, you are welcome to the comforts of this castle, but as for your marriage to my daughter, I have no desire for the nuptials to proceed. Arthur, you must proceed at once to build a force to defend our lands." With that, the king stormed from the room.

"That went well, I don't think." Matthew said out loud.

"You must remember, my young friend, most if not all the concepts and information from your world are totally foreign here and, to speak the truth, luring an army to fall into a pit which will somehow, as if by magic, open up sometime next year on a day no-one knows is a strain on one's imagination! My advice is to reconsider and hopefully devise another plan more pleasing to the king, or you may find yourself back home again— and this time forever!"

Matthew departs the Castle

Smarting from the king's rebuff of his plan, early the next morning, Matthew left the castle on horseback to scout the region outlined in the almanac.

Bethany, noting his absence at breakfast, questioned the city guards who knew of his departure but not his destination, then went to speak to her father.

"What did you say to my knight last evening, Father?" Bethany's tone was less than polite.

"Your young man is little better than a madman, my child, and, as far as I am concerned, there will be no marriage between the two of you; now fret as you will."

"Sir, you forget that not once but twice he has performed feats unheard of in our land and now, perhaps because of your unwillingness to comprehend his logic, have dismissed his plan and yes, I will now go to my quarters," storming out of the king's presence.

An unhappy Kingdom

Days passed into weeks. Arthur attempted, with scarce resources, to assemble a force capable of defending the disputed lands. The skills he saw did little to encourage him as to the outcome of any battle with the king of Powys army.

In the kingdom's east, Matthew found the valley outlined in his book. Local townsfolk sheltered and fed him; his fame as the champion dragon slayer had reached the very corners of the land. Daily, he rode the valley searching for clues as to the location of the fault line and, should the need arise, potential places where they might achieve an ambush. Unwilling to abandon his plan, he wintered in the local villages.

Bethany, furious with her father, also led a solitary existence during the cold winter months. Her nagging fear was that her true love had returned to his time forever.

Arthur returns to the Valley

It was late in January when Matthew, perched on the top of a hill overlooking the valley, felt a violent shaking, a rippling over the hills and valley. Rocks loosened by the tremor cascaded down into the valley.

Arthur, in desperation, had also come to the valley, not to seek the young knight who he suspected had returned to his own time, but to see how a battle with numerically inferior forces might be won. Travelling through the villages, talk of a lone knight came to him as he neared the region. It was early February when Arthur entered the valley; he saw many boulders that had been dislodged in recent days from the hills above. The lone figure high up also noted his presence.

"Arthur, I'm here. Climb up to the top!" Matthew called to his mentor.

Arthur, cheered by the sound of Matthew's voice, rode to find his young friend.

"Where have you been, my son? The king is much displeased, and the princess is beside herself."

"Come and sit with me, my good friend. There is something you need to consider. Each week, late on Friday afternoons, the ground is in turmoil. I'm convinced a major event is imminent, as each week the shocks are stronger. Where is the enemy force now?"

"On the march, four weeks away at the most."

Just as he finished speaking, the mountain heaved. They could see trees swaying and gaps appearing on the hillsides. "Do you see? Do you feel the power, Arthur? The book is right. It is only the timing." Matthew gripped the old man's shoulders. "Prepare the force you have and return, but say nothing to the king or Bethany concerning me or what you have witnessed here today."

Arthur, now convinced Matthew could spring a trap on the enemy force, agreed.

"Will you remain here, my son?"

"Yes, I will not leave, for better or ill. By God's grace, I will be vindicated, or die in the battle."

The Earth erupts

Starting with a growl like that of a hound, a gentle tremor rippled through the valley, growing deeper into a deafening roar that tore the valley in two. The river that ran through the middle disappeared. Thousands of terrified screams rent the air. From the top of the hill, they could see little. Only the sound of death and destruction rose from the valley floor.

With the sunrise, Arthur led his men into the valley, Matthew at his side. Enormous scars marred the landscape. The chasm that had swallowed the army had returned to its place, leaving only the shattered remnant of terrified soldiers. There was no sign of the king of Powys.

Arthur's band soon made captives of all who survived the disaster, the baggage of the invading army looted for its gold and valuables.

Matthew walked along the torn earth's scar. Looking down, he saw a glimmer of gold. Reaching into the mud, he drew out the crown of the dead king of Powys.

All day, Arthur's men collected what they could. With hundreds of captives, they made their way back into the land of Gwynedd.

The Victors return

Some days following the jubilant return of the army, Matthew made his own way into the city, riding to not draw attention to his presence.

They held a grand feast to celebrate the victory. Arthur, true to his word, never mentioned Matthew to the king or Bethany.

The king, though joyous at the defeat of his enemy, lamented his anger and rejection of the young knight and his plan, in silence sat in the great hall, Arthur and Bethany in attendance.

A soldier entered. "Sire, a young knight has entered and craves admittance."

"Who is he?" demanded the king.

"Sir Matthew, your highness, and he brings a gift."

"Matthew," the king scrambled from his throne, "send him in quickly!"

"Yes, my king."

"Matthew?" Bethany, roused from her state, leapt to her feet.

There in the doorway stood the young man from another time, unsure of his place in his own time, or this one, in his hand the crown of the king of Powys.

A joyful peace

"Your highness," he spoke as he entered the room, "I present you with the crown of the king of Powys. The earth swallowed his body, along with most of his army."

Bethany ran to Matthew and hugged him.

The king moved to greet him. "What is there I can say, my son? I am sorry to have doubted you. Now three times you have performed magnificent feats to protect me and mine; your wisdom and courage are unrivalled in the land. Apart from the hand of my daughter, what would you have as your dowery—even to half of my kingdom."

"Sire, I would claim all the disputed territories plus the castle and lands of the dragon. In controlling the contested regions, I will ensure no king of Powys or Gwynedd will fight over them ever again."

Arthur hugged his young pupil. "You have done well, young Matthew. You have made this old knight proud."

And so, Matthew and Bethany were wed, the people of the two Welsh lands now reconciled, the dragon's castle renovated by the people of Powys as a wedding gift to the newlyweds.

Through the years, they walked in peace through the forests surrounding the castle, past the pit where the slain dragon lay, but never did they pass through the forked tree again.

The Fire Fairy and the old Man

The old man had wandered the hills many times, usually alone. Looking for clues of old civilisations, old legends, old ruins.

This day he had walked further, his legs felt they were in fine condition, higher up the steep slope scrambling over moss-covered boulders he clambered until, in the late afternoon, he had to admit he was lost.

Dark shadows crept down the valley. There would not be time for him to make his way back to the car. It was more concern than fear. The concept of sleeping out on the mountains was not new to him, though it had been some years since he had slept under the stars. Now older and less subtle, his tired body preferred more comfort than the moss-covered earth would provide, and it had rained during the night.

Stopping his search for old ruins, his focus now centred on seeking a place of shelter and dry wood for a fire. It would rain again tonight, so sleeping without cover was not an option.

Pushing through some dense undergrowth, he spied a large rock outcrop jutting out further than the rest, forming a slate roof where he found comfort from the damp and cold, the ground underneath dry.

Slipping off his backpack, the search was now for kindling and other timber to keep him warm overnight. Dead leaves and small twigs were the only dry fuel he could find. He could start the fire, but without larger pieces, it would be short-lived.

Looking at the sky, he frowned, disappointed with his effort to find wood for the fire. It wasn't the lack of wood. There was plenty under every tree, but it was all sodden. He could never get them to light.

Kicking around the trees, he found a few branches he could break into smaller lengths, not enough to keep back the freezing cold. He could die on the mountainside tonight.

By now, the sun had set over the rim of the hills that hemmed in the valley. Now only the tops of the nearby mountains were in sunlight, the shadow of the rock outcrop growing darker and darker by the minute.

In desperation, he collected several wet logs. Perhaps by some miracle they would catch if dried by the smaller kindling.

His search ended with the darkness. There was nothing more he could do. Any step onto the unknown slopes would have meant injury or worse.

Squatting under the rock, he gathered the wood into a heap and managed a wry smile.

There was a legend concerning this mountain, the old folk told of a fire nymph who lived in the rocks. No one he knew had ever seen it, but that didn't stop a good folk tale.

He sighed. A fire fairy would come in handy tonight. Wrapping his coat tighter around his slim frame to keep out the damp. The meagre fire was prepared. It wasn't for cooking, there was enough food in his backpack and he would not starve before morning. No, it was for the cold.

Looking at the scant supply of wood, he thought to wait as long as he could before lighting the kindling. Pushing back into the rock wall, he shivered in the darkness. The flashlight had to be used only in an emergency.

Eventually, the shaking in his bones took control and, reaching for the matches, he struck the first one.

The flash of light almost startled him as he eased the small flame under some leaves, praying they would catch on fire. There was no point in blowing. That would only quench whatever hope the flame would have to survive and grow.

His entire being was focused on the fate of the leaf. The match flame licked the underside of a large brown leaf, then died. The leaf would not cooperate.

Disappointment is not the term you would use when, in the icy darkness, a fire will not start.

Though not a confirmed stoic, the old man had learned many of life's hard lessons. He fumbled back into the small box to retrieve another match. With increasing hope, he placed the small flame under the same leaf, hoping residual heat would have made it more susceptible to ignition.

Smiling, he saw the leaf crackle and burst into flame. Tenderly, he placed strands of grass over the burning leaf. The tiny flame remained. Easing a twig over the flickering grass, it too soon burned.

So engrossed in the fire's birth, a small glow from the overhanging rock escaped his notice.

Soft orange eyes peered from a crack in the rock face. She had a visitor.

Her life was separate from mortals. She held no compassion for, nor fear of the old man. From the security of her place above his head, she watched his desperate attempt to create what she was made of — fire.

Few mortals ventured near her home, still less dared to overnight in her presence. She had heard talk of an old man wandering the hills, digging, scratching, photographing old aspects of the ridge. Pondering his visage, she felt she may have seen him once or twice, but not here, not alone, lost and cold.

Leaf by leaf, twig by twig, the fire grew.

Gently larger and larger pieces were laid on to the flames, fearful he would smother the flame and with no more kindling there would be no fire that night.

Eventually, he relaxed. The flames rose gleefully in the frosty night air, shafts of heat slowly radiated into his stiff hands.

Reaching into his bag, he drew out a ham sandwich, not as fresh as it was this morning, but under the circumstances, he received the food with thanks.

Despite the relief that the fire was established, his lingering fear that the dry wood soon would be exhausted, he eased the damp logs closer and closer, hoping that the fire would dry them enough they would catch and his comfort would be secured.

Sadly, as most things are wont to do, the fire's embers were not enough to thaw the damp logs and, minute by minute, the radiant warmth sagged and slumped back into the rock on which it had been laid.

He moved closer to the dying embers, trying to attract what warmth remained. There was nothing else he could do. Tired, cold and alone, the old man whispered a last prayer and fell asleep.

Convinced she would not be discovered, the fire fairy flew from her home and hovered over the head of the old man. She had heard his last heart felt prayer, indeed if she did nothing, he would be dead by morning. The freezing cold on the mountain would ensure that.

Sitting on a burning twig, she looked into his face. Was he a good man, or an evil man, she could not tell. But here he was in her care.

She had no concept of death, she just was. Yet, she knew humans were not like her. They came, and they went. Perhaps that was why she was indifferent at first to the plight of her guest.

A damp twig popped in the flame. The old man woke with a start. There, right in front of him, sat a tiny figure. "I must be dreaming or hallucinating from the cold," he thought.

She put a finger to her lips for him to be silent, nodding; he fell back into a fitful sleep.

She liked his eyes; they were the eyes of someone seeking after the truth. She decided he would not die here tonight.

Flying behind the sodden logs, she pushed them onto the lingering flames, flapping her wings, they fanned the fire to engulf the logs. Steam and smoke rose from the fire pit, then in an instant the wet logs burst into flame.

Heat radiated from the logs, warming the old man, who rolled away, the heat more than he needed for comfort.

All night the fire fairy brought logs for the fire to keep the old man comfortable. A deep frost formed on the mountainside. Nothing unprotected would survive the harsh chill of the winter's night.

Sitting on a log, she watched him sleep in peace. For some strange reason, she felt happier than she had in centuries. The fire burned bright all night, and as the sun's first glow struggled over the mountain tops, the old man woke.

There in front of him burned a robust fire. Groaning in pain, he stretched and sat trying to warm his body. As he looked into the fire, he stopped, there on a log, in the middle of the fire, the tiny girl from his dream of last night.

Struggling to get as close to the flames as he dared, he stared at her; her smiling face beamed back in radiant red and orange, almost invisible in the flames.

"Thank you," he mouthed.

Then, like a spark from the centre of the fire, she floated upward into the morning sunlight and was gone.

The Town Sweeper

Nestled at the end of a long green valley, it was just another country town, perhaps a thousand people, no more. Most worked on the land, lived healthy and contented lives; but there was one thing they were always concerned about.

The town, though, had few children seen playing in the streets. It wasn't they weren't being born, it's just that, from time to time, they disappeared. One by one without a trace, usually between five and thirteen years old, boys and girls alike.

After every disappearance, the town folk would search for days trying to find the child, but they had always gone without a trace.

It was not on any particular night or season, their disappearance seemed quite random. The parents, when questioned, did not know why their child should be taken. Rumours that the child was a little 'hard to handle' had been often heard in the town.

Every night after the townsfolk had left their businesses, the cattle safe in their barns, and all the children safe indoors, the town sweeper started his rounds.

All evening, he would pass from house to house, keeping the town's paths and streets clear and clean. All were grateful for the service he performed, though no one knew him; they just remembered his courteous manner.

Outside the town, a mile or so away from the last house, on the top of a small rise, stood a clump of oak trees. Many tales were connected with the trees, none were pleasant. Some said that when the wind blew from the North, moans and sighs could be heard coming from the hill; others told that when the moon was full, the sound of children crying could be heard.

Such suspicion being heaped on the trees meant no-one ever went there after dark, and it would be a brave man to pass through there even in daylight. All preferred to skirt the trees should they need to travel that way.

At sun-set, the sweeper would wind his way through the town, sweeping up leaves and rubbish left by the people. He would make his way past the houses of the town, the only sound that of the straw broom on the cobbles.

As he would pass a house, he would stop and listen, and, when he heard the sounds of a settled family, would smile and walk on. Should though, angry cries of discontent be heard, he would listen further, leaning closer to the door, and, if the sharp words came from the mouth of a child he would frown, shake his head and walk past the door, only to return late at night to sweep the child out of the house and away beyond the town.

There, fear struck, the child, with outstretched hands, would be turned into an oak tree, its branches drooping in despair, like those of the naughty offspring. It would not matter to the sweeper if the child was a boy or girl, if he had heard nastiness, a raised voice or disobedience, it was all the same to him, every one would be changed.

Come morning, the cries of the parents would be heard throughout the village; all knew what had happened. The spoiled behaviour of the child would have been well known. Some indeed considered that this was why they had been taken, though no one knew how, or why, or by whom.

Year after year, naughty and rebellious children were taken away; all parents warned their children what may befall them, but sadly, few listened.

At each and every full moon, as the soft glow rose over the mountains, there, deep in the wood, trees turned back into the same child that had been taken, all at the same age as when they had been removed from the town.

Wide-eyed, they would walk to the centre of the woods where they could mix and talk amongst themselves; the sweeper would stand back, listening to their talk.

Almost always, they fell into bitter complaint over their lot, angry at being removed and transformed; the sweeper looked on sadly. But, now and again; though seldom, one child would lament the wickedness it had done while in the village, and, with genuine remorse, repented of their behaviour.

The keen ears of the sweeper detected this change of heart, and smiling, would take the sorry child outside the ring of the trees. Once he and the child had come away, the others, all unrepentant, were turned back into oaks, there to await the next full moon.

At precisely 6 am the following morning, the remorseful child would appear in the town square, just next to the old fountain; neither moving nor crying out. Patient and still, it waited for the sunrise, hoping to be reunited with its parents.

Parents of children who had been taken all knew that on the morning following a full moon a child might have returned, so they gathered in the early morning light, hundreds of desperate mothers and fathers would enter the square in the hope their child had been restored.

Of course, many years may have passed, and though the child had not aged, the parents had. Some had moved away, while for some, it had been so long they had grown old, and some had even died.

Eager, the anxious crowd would circle the child, hoping it was theirs; sometimes it would be very hard to even recognise their own offspring because of the passage of time. With down-cast eyes, many returned to their homes, their child still missing. However; if no-one claimed the child, it would start a piteous begging and plead with the remaining couples to take it home, promising on its life to be obedient and cheerful. From one couple to another, it would go, until a spark of love grew between them and the child; never was such a child left standing alone in the square.

Standing afar off, the sweeper stood. Saddened to still see so many grieving parents, but on this day, his old heart warmed as he watched the returned child walk home, hand in hand with its new parents.

A Gift for the King

Once upon a time, there was a land that seemed to flow with milk and honey. The olive tree grew, and no child went hungry.

A noble king had ruled for a long time. H had ascended the throne following the death of his father in the final horrific battle to win the war against the evil barbarians who had plundered the coast lines for a generation.

Each year, on a day set aside to honour the last king, there was a parade and festival. Everyone dressed in their most colourful clothing. The day would be a time of rejoicing. On his splendid white horse, the King would ride through the streets, his crisp black suit and gold chains glittering in the sun, cheering children would throw red and yellow rose petals onto the cobbles as he rode past.

At the castle gate, a crowd would form for what had become the most special part of the day's festivities. Precisely at noon the king would sit, surrounded by his loyal band of soldiers, then to allow, just for the one hour each year, any of his subjects to approach with a request or grievance.

It had become a tradition that betrothed couples would approach the king, hoping to receive a blessing and a token of his royal favour. This year, two couples drew near to the king's throne, and with much clapping and cheering of their friends and family, they approached. The king, with a warm smile, gave each a gold coin and his best wishes for the future.

Behind the four lovers stood an old man, before him, held close, a boy, almost concealed by his grimy brown coat. As the joyous couples moved away from the throne, there, standing quietly and still, the old man and the boy waited.

Guards, seeing the dishevelled old man, sought to remove him from the king's presence, but with a stay of the king's hand, they remained still.

The king's eyes, spotting the boy almost hidden in front of the gnarled form of the man, beckoned the pair to come forward. The crowd, dismissive, sneered at the disrespect showed to the king, their rags an insult to the festive nature of the day.

"What would you have, friend?" asked the king

The old man, who could scarce look upon the king, his state an affront to the proceedings, stepped forward. "My king, some ten years ago, while walking by the river, I found an abandoned child wrapped in tattered clothes at the point of death. Not knowing what to do, yet as an honest man, I could not leave the child to die, so I took it home and have raised the lad to this day. My king, I am at death's door and can no longer care for the boy." Then the old man leant forward closer to the king's ear, "Sire, the boy is special, he sees into the future, everything he has ever told me has come to pass, would you accept him as a gift from me and from his unknown parents."

The blue eyes of the boy sparkled. The king sat perplexed and gazed at the young child. Before he could answer, the old man collapsed at the feet of the king and died. The boy now left standing alone, twice abandoned.

A hush came over the crowd. Some rushed to assist the old man, but he had died as he fell to the ground.

Rising to his feet, the king summoned his guards to bring the old man's body and the child into the castle; the celebrations were over.

Though all the people loved the king, he was without an heir. The king was not against marriage and desired a son to follow him. It was that he had not found the right one, though many kings of neighbouring lands had sought an alliance. Their daughters were all turned down, though politely.

The king sent messengers to collect the boy's belongings from the old man's cottage. Their simple life meant he had not much more than the clothes he stood in, with no clue as to his actual parents found. The king's servants sealed the doors and windows, leaving its fate to another time.

The boy, though not having said a word since entering the castle, was washed and dressed in neat new clothes, hurriedly sourced from the town's tailor. Taken into the kitchen, the cook and the serving girls fed him. His clear blue eyes took in all the features and fixings in the kitchen, the penetrating gaze searched out the women in the room, never had he been in the contact of women prior to this time nor had he spoken to one in his entire life.

"Do you have a name?" the cook asked as she placed the bowl of steaming meat broth in front of him. Shaking his head, he picked up the spoon and ate. The women knew of the dramatic events leading to the boy's presence. Rumours like falcons flew through the castle.

Everyone wondered what the king would do with the boy.

The king had not forgotten about the lad. However, the pressures of the kingdom meant he had not yet tried to speak to the boy. After breakfast the following morning, the king walked into his study. There, on the floor, surrounded by books, sat the young boy. Silently, he stood and watched as the young lad scoured through the pages like someone frantically searching for a lost treasure. It was some time before the boy sensed the king's presence. Unsure what to do, but unafraid, he looked up from the floor into the face of the king, and now his protector.

Walking to where the boy sat, the king knelt beside him, picked up a volume to see what the interest was for the boy. "Do you read son?" the king asked, not an unusual request as they schooled few country folk.

"Yes sir, my father taught me," he replied.

"Do you mean the old man that brought you yesterday?"

"Yes sir, he was the only father I have known, though he always said I had another father before him."

"Well son, we have many volumes here for you to read, though we will have to find a better place for your endeavours than my study floor," the king smiled. The king's father and his father before had, at great expense over many years, collected a vast library so he was pleased to have someone reading them.

"What is your name?" asked the king.

"I don't have one sir, my father said it was not his place to name me. He called me 'son'."

"Well, if you are to live here, you will need a name other than 'son'. Have you ever thought about what name you would like to have?"

"I have always liked George, sir," the boy replied.

"Then George you shall be; you will need more names than that, but for now one will be enough." Smiling again, the king walked to his desk, leaving the boy, who turned back to the pile of books.

Distracted by the boy's presence, the king sat and watched as young George went from book to book, yet carefully, as if aware of their worth.

Recalling the words of the old man that the boy was special, the king sought the wisest men to tutor the lad in sciences and languages. Within a month, they had prepared new quarters where George both lived and learned from men of great skill and intellect. Daily tutored in Latin, Greek, mathematics, and history, his intellect grew, social graces were not forgotten, riding, archery and hunting filled the remaining time.

Soon, the lad was a constant companion of the king. On all formal outings he walked at the side of the king, as if a son not a servant, a prince in all but name.

Some time later, over dinner, the boy, now growing in stature and wisdom, spoke, "My king, I fear, unless you move the people living near the river to higher ground, there will be a substantial loss of life."

The king's eyes now fixed on George; he dismissed the servants from the room. "Go on my son," He and George now the room's only occupants.

"Sire, this coming winter will be exceedingly severe, leading to tremendous snowfall on the mountains, which when melted in spring will flood the land destroying many houses and bridges, urgently you must build new dwellings and even to the planning of a new town."

"How do you know this? The town has never flooded in living memory?"

"My king," George replied, "I have both read in the land's history and in my studies of the seasons, and above all, sir, I have a foreboding in my head and heart, which I cannot explain."

The king sat, gazing still into the clear bright eyes of the young man sitting across the table from him. He had received reports of George spending time along the banks of the river and around the houses of the town built near the water.

"How long have you felt this way?"

"My understanding and fears have grown over the last month, sir, but I would not venture to discuss this with you until they drew me to this conclusion."

"Do you have a plan, George?"

"Yes, my king, I have drawn up charts and maps of the changes needed both to save lives and improve the well-being of the people."

The king smiled. What had the old man said, that the boy would be a gift?

Work began at once. All available men under the leadership of young George, none questioned his authority. A few of the townsfolk living near the river were unhappy about being moved, unaware of their danger, but with the king's soldiers at his side, the work proceeded.

For months, the work went on. Finally, as winter approached, the new houses were complete, a stronger, higher bridge constructed to span the river, plus improved roads, making the town more efficient and grand.

The bitter cold winter lay heavy on the land. Snow and frost kept most indoors. Never had the people seen such a time. George looked over the snow-laden mountains, his inner feelings troubling him, though he knew the towns would be secure.

Spring came, and the snow melted, flood waters roared through the valleys. Trees near the watercourse ripped up by the roots formed battering rams, spearing their way down rivers and streams, smashing bridges and destroying anything in their path.

Stories filtered into the castle from nearby kingdoms of horrendous losses, hundreds of deaths through injury and drowning, massive damage to buildings and bridges.

The king, with George at his side, inspected the floods as they careered through the town. A torrent of water, at a level never seen before, gouged stretches of banks as the water surged down the valley.

People moved to higher ground were now very thankful. Throughout the land, the talk was now only of the floods and of George.

With the king's blessing, George undertook changes to the way the people farmed, bringing in new seeds from other lands; wheat, barley, corn and other plants good for food and clothing. Soon, these crops flourished under his guidance. The land soon grew rich as other kingdoms came to buy.

On the king's birthday, they held a grand party. Kings, queens, princesses, and princes from many lands came to join the festivities. The banquet was in keeping with the status of the host and his guests. Those present, all in resplendent attire, sat around the tables with the king at the head, George at his side.

Near the end of the proceedings, the king called for silence. "My dear guests, friends, one and all, I have an announcement to make. This land of mine over recent years has grown rich and prosperous, a thing we have all benefited by, a time of blessing for our lands and peoples, this happy state of affairs I would have it known largely brought about through the skill and endeavours of this young man at my side. It is, therefore, with a glad heart tonight, before all these witnesses, I declare him my adopted son and heir to the crown." The king then took off his royal ring and placed it on George's finger.

Cheering and clapping broke out in the hall, the formal nature of the event broken. Kings with marriageable daughters scrambled for introductions to the now Prince George.

The king leaned close to George and whispered in his ear. "You have another name now, son, mine."

As crown prince, George's status flourished far and wide, his wisdom, learning and foresight made him sought after by all the neighbouring lands. Any king who possessed a beautiful princess pursued a match. Each king vying with his neighbour, offering splendid inducements to secure the marriage.

Prince George, now more worldly wise, his gift of insight well developed, finally agreed to wed the most beautiful and gifted princess, her dowry, her father's kingdom.

On the night before his wedding, the king and George sat together in the grand library. A warm fire flickered in the dim light. "My son," the king looked at his heir, "do you remember how it was living with the old man, and do you remember what he said when you stood before me on the bridge?"

"Yes father, he was poor but learned, he owned a few books which he prized. With these he taught me to read and so gained understanding. When walking, he would show me wonderful things out of the world's splendour; and yes, I also remember what he said shortly before he died. Why I am blessed with certain understandings I do not know, but this much I realise, that now I have had three fathers, and that is enough for any man."

The Girl by the Bridge

It was always dark under the bridge; but that wasn't the only reason he never ventured near the dull grey stones that formed the arch.

There was a story in the town of a girl with long brown hair who had been playing along the bank one summer's day when her ball fell into the water, she had waded into the cold stream to fetch it, followed it under the arch and disappeared.

The men of the village searched the clear waters, thinking the girl must have tripped in the dark and drowned; carrying torches, they scoured the area, but found no sign of her. Not even the ball had come out the other side of the bridge.

That was back when his grandfather was a young man, or so his father had told him. But no one let their children play near the bridge from that time on.

Despite the warnings, it was his habit to play or just sit on the bank near the opening of the bridge. In fact, you could almost always find him there most summer afternoons after school. Choosing solitude over soccer, reading over rugby, or, as his mother would say, fantasy over reality.

The taunts of the other children never ruffled his moods, content within himself, the playful gurgling of the stream enough company as he read in the late afternoon.

"Hello," a voice called to him. It was a girl who had somehow come and sat beside him.

Roused from his book, he looked at her. She seemed familiar somehow, and yet he could not remember ever seeing her before, or even anyone like her. Her long brown hair, soft grey eyes, and pleasant voice engaged him.

"Hello," was all he could say. He was not comfortable around girls, especially if alone with one. Still, afraid of appearing rude, he continued, "do you live in the village?"

"I used to," she replied.

"Oh," Somehow feeling uncomfortable in her presence and yet attracted to her, he said, "I often sit here and read."

"Yes," came the reply.

"Well, I'd best be going," he scrambled to his feet, looked down at her now sad face, and headed off home. Before he turned the corner near the post office, he looked back. But she had gone.

Every day he sat and read in the afternoon sun, every day hoping; despite his nature, she would come and sit by him again. There was something in her eyes, those soft grey eyes, that beaconed him to move closer, to let her closer, perhaps to let him closer. The week passed in its usual solitude, the memory of her fading with the late afternoon sun.

It was Monday of the following week. Summer would soon turn to autumn. The sun set lower each day; the leaves trying to stay green, the air crisper than the day before.

He shivered in the late afternoon.

"Hello."

He turned and smiled at her. "I'm so glad you came back. I can't say why, but I hoped you would come back and sit with me again."

"I'm glad you still come and sit," she replied.

They sat and watched the water flow down the stream, then disappear out of sight under the bridge.

"Are you cold?" he asked, seeing her shiver in the late afternoon.

"A little. I always feel the cold."

Taking his jacket, he draped it around her shoulders. She took his book and leafed through the pages.

"Do you like to read?" he asked.

"I used to," then turning to him, took off his coat and handed it back, "you'd better go now, it's late."

"But will you be all right?" he looked into her soft grey eyes.

"You must leave now." Was all she said. He sensed a coldness in her voice, as if a warning.

"Will you be here tomorrow?" his desire was obvious.

"Possibly, I can't tell."

Rising from beside her, he put his jacket back on and headed home. Before reaching the corner, he turned; hoping to see her still sitting on the bank, hoping to see her smile, wave to him, but she was not there.

"Where have you been!" his mother asked, "you will catch a death of cold being out so late."

The blue of summer turned to the gold of autumn and, day by day, to the grey of winter; like the grey of her eyes.

With coat, gloves, hat, and scarf, he sat by the stream; he never even knew her name, but that was unimportant. They were, in some unknown way, bound.

The trees, now naked, stood by the stream; the late afternoon sun from when he first saw her now turned to the dull grey of impending darkness. As the days passed, he no longer sat. He just slowed and stood for a while, waiting, hoping she would see him.

It was a long winter, made longer by his desire to see the girl once more.

Soon though, as is the nature of things, the trees budded and the days grew longer and warmer.

Again, he sat on the bank of the stream near the bridge, often reading, though sometimes just looking into the water as it rushed down from the mountains, then disappear into the blackness under the bridge. Summer having arrived, his expectations of her return grew.

"Hello," she smiled and sat down next to him on the bank.

Excited to see her, he turned and smiled. She seemed just the same as last summer; her long hair flowed over her shoulders as the water flowed over the rocks in the stream, her grey eyes soft, yet sad.

"Did you go away for the winter?" he asked.

"Not really." The reply asking more questions than it answered. It was clear she would not divulge any personal information.

Together, they sat and watched the water flow under the bridge, saying nothing. Unsure, he reached out his hand to take hers; hoping a physical contact would do what words seemed incapable of doing.

"Best not to." She said, watching his hand move closer to her own.

"But I like you," he blurted out.

"Like me, how can you like me? You know nothing about me." Her blunt response to his approach, a door slamming in his face.

"I would like to get to know you," he persisted.

"Perhaps, but not yet," she looked at him, "you should leave now."

Her words dismissed the boy. He rose, smiled, and walked to the corner. Happy to see her again, yet saddened and a little disturbed by her words and her response to his advances.

Many days later, she returned. She seemed in high spirits, something he had not seen before. Now, her reserve seemed gone and his hopes of love surfaced.

They chatted for a few minutes before she said, "Will you play with me? I have brought my ball."

He looked at her. For someone so reserved, catching a ball seemed out of character. Still, he would not dampen any romantic union that may develop.

"Sure," he replied, "what do you want to do?"

"You stand by the bank," she suggested. "I'll stand back here a little and we can throw the ball to each other."

Instantly complying, he stood with his back to the water, watching her as she stepped back about six paces, turned and threw the ball to him.

Catching it, he saw the smile on her face, like that of a little child playing. Gently he threw the ball back to her. Once more, she threw it to him and again he returned it to the girl.

Her smile faded. "One more time!" she called and threw the ball way over his outstretched hands, landing in the stream twenty yards from the bridge.

"My ball, my ball!" she cried. "You must fetch my ball!"

Afraid of disappointing her, he pulled off his shoes and socks and waded into the stream. The swift current was taking the ball closer to the bridge.

"You must save my ball!" she cried out to him.

Heedless of the warnings and his own fears, he chased the ball through the chill knee-deep water, stumbling over the stones, desperate to retrieve the ball before it went under the arch of the bridge.

"Hurry, hurry!" she cried out again.

Now obsessed with securing the ball, he barely noticed passing under the bridge's arch and into the blackness beyond.

His parents alerted the police when he did not arrive home after school; "He sits by the bridge reading," his mother told the officers. They searched the area for days but found no trace. An old lady who lived near the bridge thought she had seen him playing ball with a girl she could not recognise; "Long brown hair she had," she told police.

Beyond the Wall

She tried not to move, staring out of the window at the passing countryside. More apprehensive than afraid, a small water bottle clutched tight in her hands. She could sense the eyes in the mirror from time to time as he looked back at his passenger.

"We are approaching a rest area, Miss. Georgia, would you care to stop?"

"I'm fine, thank you." She replied, not looking into his eyes.

It was late afternoon when they arrived. The maid attended the car as soon as the wheels stopped, stepping back as the driver opened the rear door.

"Hello Miss Georgia, how lovely to have you come and stay with us. Let me take you to your room. Your grandmother will join you for dinner."

With just a nod, the girl climbed out of the Daimler, smiled at the driver, who held the door open, and followed the white uniformed maid inside. Unlike anything she had ever seen, the manor house had seven bedrooms, all with baths, three formal rooms, two dining rooms, kitchen, staff quarters, stables, and various outbuildings.

Georgia tried not to stare as she followed the girl through the marble floored rooms and up the winding stairs to the private suites.

"Your grandmother thought this room would suit. It overlooks the garden and catches the morning sun." She smiled.

"Thank you."

"My name is Lucy, I hope we can become friends," and held out her hand.

"That would be nice. Thank you, Lucy. I'm Georgia."

"Would you like me to put your things away?"

"I can do it." The young girl protested.

"As you wish, if you need me, just press the green button on the wall. Dinner will be at eight. I'll come and get you at seven forty-five. Would you care for a bath before dinner?" The girl nodded. "Then let me show you how it all works."

The maid turned back to see her young charge sitting on the bed, her head low, crying.

"Miss Georgia, what's the matter?"

"I'm sorry, but I don't know what I am supposed to do. This house is so large, and I only have two dresses to wear."

"I tell you what," she moved to sit beside the girl, "let's have a nice bath and then you and I can pick which dress would be best for you to wear for dinner. I understand you will go shopping tomorrow, so then you will have a fine assortment of lovely clothes to wear."

Nodding at the suggestion, though concerned with what tomorrow would bring, Georgia tried to settle into her quarters.

"All ready? The smiling face entered the room. Dinner is about to be served, so we need to get you seated. Your grandmother doesn't like to wait."

"I'm ready. Do I look all right?"

"You look just fine. Remember, you live here now, you are family, so please try to relax."

The two made their way in silence down the stairs and into the dining room. Georgia looked around, trying to get her bearings, trying to work out how to get from A to B.

"Sit here, Miss. Georgia, that way you can talk to your grandmother and not have to raise your voice."

Another nod, another piece of the puzzle put into place.

The room became silent as Lucy retreated into the kitchen. Georgia played with the silver knife, fork, and spoon. Smiling as she could see her reflection, though distorted, in the glistening utensils.

A looming shadow made her jump in fear.

"Oh child, I'm so sorry to have startled you. Come and give me a hug. Look at you, so much bigger than the last time we were together."

As she faced the shadow, now transformed into her grandmother, she tried to smile, replaced the spoon on the table and stood. "Thank you for letting me come and live with you, grandmother."

The old woman ignored the child's pleasantries and grasped the young girl in her arms.

"I'm so sad this has been such a troublesome time, Georgia. Nothing we can say or do will turn back the clock. We, you and I, are going to have to learn to get along with one another. No doubt we will have our challenges, but always remember, dear, I love you so very much."

Georgia's arms now reached around the old lady and hugged.

"Shall I plate up, madam?" The butler's voice broke them apart.

"Yes, thank you. Come, Georgia, let's sit and eat. Then you can tell me all about your trip here and I'll tell you what I have planned to help you settle in. Would that be all right?"

"Yes, of course, thank you."

Though hungry, Georgia was mindful not to appear so. Following her grandmother's lead, she cut and chewed with as much precision as a ten-year-old could manage.

Dessert being served, the conversation began. "Tell me dear, how was your journey, and are you happy with the room I have selected for you?"

"Your car is very comfortable, grandmother, and quiet."

The old lady laughed, "Yes, it is, isn't it. And your room, do you like the view from the window? Do you know that when I was a little girl like you that was my room, I loved to look out over the garden."

"It's beautiful. I'm sure I will be happy there."

"Tomorrow, you and I are going shopping. I fear you need a change of wardrobe, not that your dress isn't delightful, but times have moved on, or so they have informed me." She laughed again.

Georgia looked at her but said nothing.

"Well, dear, I expect you need to rest after your long trip, so let's say good night now. I'll see you for breakfast here at eight. Can you find your own way back to your room?"

"Yes, thank you, grandmother, and thank you for the meal. Goodnight."

Alone, she sat in the bay window, looking out over the garden. Lights shone inside the walls, making it seem like a fairyland. The water fountain droplets sparkled with the reflection.

Another light caught her eye. There, over the wall, over the meadow and into the woods, she could see a glow. It meandered through the trees, stopping from time to time, then moved on. Georgia, fascinated, forgot to change and go to bed. A knock on the door startled her.

"Are you all right, Miss. Georgia, I thought you would be asleep." The maid, under strict instructions, was to manage the young visitor as she adjusted to her new surroundings.

"Sorry, Lucy, I was just watching the light in the woods."

"Hunters, I suspect. Come on now, you have had a big day and tomorrow will be the same, so you need to sleep. I'll wake you for breakfast. Sleep well."

"Goodnight Lucy, thank you."

Daily, the conversations with her grandmother diminished, left to the tutor and house staff, Georgia's routine settled into daily schooling, afternoons in the garden, dining alone and evenings looking out of her window toward the woods, over the gardens, beyond the wall.

At one corner of the garden stood an oak tree, its branches sweeping over both the garden beds and, as Georgia soon realised, over the wall.

Summer came into the garden. Blossoms filled every inch of space with colour and fragrance. Sometimes Georgia saw her grandmother walking through the flowers with the old gardener by her side. It was the only place where the young girl could run and play, though the gardener was never happy should she trip and fall into a garden bed. Despite one or two falls, she had managed to climb the tree. She would sit in the join of two large branches and look out over the meadow and into the woods. The summer breeze brought wonderful sounds to her ears.

Sweet sounds, odd sounds, and if she strained to listen, she could hear a rippling brook. One evening, sitting by the open window, the pale glow appeared in the trees. Now, not just the sounds of the forest could be heard, but what she felt was a voice calling her name.

At first, she just smiled, thinking it to be a jumble of other sounds that, when all put together, sounded like 'Georgia'. But when the sound repeated her name over and over, she became afraid, closed the window and went to bed, pulling the blankets right over her head.

All night she dreamed and the call of the voice continued, unsure if the sounds were just in her dreams or real. The voice was soft as a mother's voice. Was it her mother's voice she wondered as she woke?

All that day she felt an urge, a desire to leave the beautiful garden and the splendid house. She wanted to be free, to run and jump beyond the walls. She wanted to find the voice, but she didn't know why.

Perched high in the oak tree, her eyes wandered over the garden, the meadow, and the woods. Looking down, she spied Lucy slipping along the edge of the wall toward the garden gate. Georgia thought it odd the maid had not used the pathway. She sat and watched as Lucy unlocked the gate and eased through the wall. Leaning out further, Georgia could see Lucy meet a young man and was soon embracing and kissing him. The couple pushed hard against the wall to avoid being seen.

The sound of a tinkling bell startled the young lovers, and the girl engrossed in watching their antics. Lucy rushed from the arms of her lover, back through the garden and into the house, neglecting to shut the gate. Georgia laughed, thinking how Lucy had almost been caught kissing a boy.

Climbing down, she looked to see if the old gardener was watching and, seeing no one, eased toward the gate and squeezed through. The gate squeaked as she tried to close it just enough so everyone in the house would think it closed. With no sound of alarm, and only the sound of the voice in her head, she headed off over the meadow towards the dark wood.

It was not as dark as it had seemed from her window or the tree. Unsure but determined, she passed the tree line. As she moved deeper into the woods, the glow she had seen night after night seemed to dance between the trunks of the trees and came closer.

"Hello Georgia, I'm so glad you came."

"How do you know my name?" She asked the glowing ball.

"I know all about you and your grandmother."

"Do you know my mother and father also?"

"No, they never lived here, but I am sad you are alone."

"You said you knew my grandmother. How?"

"Well, when she was very young, she came to find me, just as you have. But she only came to visit once."

"Is that why she is so old?"

"No," the voice laughed, "it was many years ago."

"Was she afraid as I am?"

"Yes, but you mustn't be. You are quite safe here."

An odd warmth swept over the girl. She stopped and sat on the soft grass as the light danced around and around, coming closer to where she sat, stopping just a few feet in front of her staring eyes. Peering deep into the light, Georgia saw what seemed to be a lady.

"Who are you?" she asked as she stared.

"It's a little hard to explain, but I am the spirit of the woods. I look after all the trees, the stream, the animals, the fish in the water and if you will let me, I will also take care of you as well."

"Did my grandmother let you look after her?"

"No, she wanted more than I could give. She wanted to be rich, to own a big house with lots of servants. I don't work like that."

"She has all these things, but I think she is still sad."

"Yes, the things she wanted, and now has, can never give you true peace and happiness."

"But I am young and don't yet know what I want in my life. Perhaps it was too hard for her to understand what you were telling her."

"Perhaps. With me dealing only with the woods and all the things that are in it, they find it easy and a comfort. You humans are much more complicated."

"I don't mean to be."

"Then what do you want, Georgia?"

"I like to play and run and jump."

"Is that all?"

"I think so. Should I want more, and if so, what should I seek after?"

"The trees seek growth and long life; the stream wants to run and the fish want to jump. If I gave you what they desire, you would become bored very soon. You need more than the folk here."

"What?"

The glow grew and grew. The tiny image became larger and larger until she was a full-grown woman, shining with a blue and green dress that reached down to her feet. "Give me your hand child, I would like to show you some things."

Georgia stood and felt the warmth of the hand of the spirit of the woods.

The trees all nodded, respecting the spirit as they walked. The animals all followed along behind. Georgia turned to see the procession of little creatures and smiled.

"We give you the power to lead, to govern with wisdom, to encourage but not dominate, to guide but not oppress all these, and the inanimate things. Nothing and no one is here by chance."

"Will you help me? I am just a little girl."

"Today you are, but tomorrow you will be a woman, a leader in the county. As for your request, yes, I will always be here should you need or want my help."

As they returned to the edge of the woods, Georgia felt the hand remove from hers. Turning, the lady had vanished. Only the warm glow remained.

"Return now. Much has changed since you came to visit. Rule well."

Walking over the meadow, everything seemed smaller, shorter, but as she could not see herself, she had no idea of what had happened in the woods.

The garden gate was wide open as she approached. Once inside, she noticed a young man tending the garden, who smiled and nodded as she approached. "Was your walk in the woods pleasant, madam?"

She smiled at him and walked toward the house, where a maid waited on the steps. "Where would you care to eat lunch, madam?"

"Here, so I can smell the blossoms." She turned to see her reflection in the glass doors. She was no longer a little girl, but a grown woman.

There was no sign of her grandmother or any of the staff she had remembered.

A new generation, one to replace the one gone before.

Daily she walked across the meadow and into the woods, a place no longer dark and foreboding. The sun shone through the branches and a soft, warm glow led the way.

Moonlight and the Lake Fairy

His grandfather had told him many times that, on a full moon in Autumn, when the wind was still; if you are very patient, quiet, and have a pure heart, something wonderful would happen at the lake.

"Did it ever happen to you, Grandad?" he asked.

"Once, when I was very young, a little like you; before the cares of the world clouded my mind, before the sights and sounds of other things drowned out what nature intended, we should hold dear."

"Could you ever see it again, Grandad?"

"I would give a king's ransom to see it, my boy. But once we break the magic of purity, it can never be made whole again." The boy noticed a tear in the old man's eye.

"Will you come with me?" he asked.

"No, my child, you and you alone must wait by the lake. You must not be impatient, you must not become cross or want things to be just the way you want, you must accept what the night gives and be thankful."

These memories he stored all summer long. The sadness of his grandfather's death caused the boy much grief. The old man was not just his grandfather, he was his link to another time, another place. A place where magic happened. Could the story he had been told of a time a hundred years ago still be true now?

He had gone to the lake many times, always when the moon was full.

He had waited for hours; nothing happened. Perhaps the breeze had caused too many ripples on the water, he was never sure.

The boy had spoken to his father. Had he ever been there? Had he ever seen anything? It was just an old man's imagination; his father told him. Don't go getting all confused with stuff that has no business being part of our life.

He loved the woods that surrounded the house. Left to his own devices, he would spend hours walking through the Fir and Birch. Now and then he would spy a stag pulling up some roots through the fallen leaves and branches. They would look at one another, no sound, no fear; until either the boy or the Stag would wander off, leaving the other alone.

The days grew colder, gold and brown replaced the green of the Birch. In a month or two, they would be just bare sticks, naked in the snow until the sun returned.

Each night after supper, he would walk to the lake, looking up at the moon and down into the water. It had to be just right, his grandfather had said, not one ripple, and the moon was bright and full.

It was early November. Brown and gold leaves littered the forest floor. The old stag used his antlers to shift away the foliage to expose the last of the green tipped shoots. They were only a few feet apart when the boy spotted the eyes glowing in the sunset.

Having eaten, it was the boy's role to walk away, leaving the other to fossick for his dinner.

The lake was like glass. Not a murmur or ripple disturbed the surface. His heart racing, he turned to look to the east, to the rising of the moon. Late autumn was cold; in the morning the ground would crackle underfoot, the frost lingering until late afternoon. But now, sitting still beside the water with the damp descending, he shivered in the cold, calm air. Was this the time? He wondered?

A swan moved on the water. Tiny waves spread from her passage. With a casual glance towards the boy, nothing more, she moved on, as silent as the ripples that made their way to the shore. He watched them fold, one after another, onto the stones, and, one by one, they disappeared from view.

With his attention focused on the swan, he almost forgot about the moon. Above the tallest fir trees, a light shone. Shadows formed on the water; dark formless shapes of the forest drifted over the surface. The night's lesser light moved to cast its glow over the lake.

The boy had found a rock to sit on, some solid ground on which to base his long hoped for, dreamt of, experience.

Feeling a warm breath on his neck, he turned to see the stag standing right behind him, he too looking out onto the water, watching, waiting.

The boy's breath hung in the air like a cloud, the silence broken only by the Stag's rhythmical breathing. The soft, low tone was a baseline for the magic to be unfolded.

A large fallen tree glowed in the moonlight, more than the moon's glow, as if a new light shone from behind it. He had never seen blue light before. Soon, like a blue fire, it rose from behind the tree.

Inches from the water, flashes of blue and white traced an arc towards the Stag and the boy. A tiny flying creature, its wings dipping at each beat into the surface of the lake, the moon shining onto the expanding ripples made by the tips of tiny wings. A blue and silver trail formed over the water as the nymph circled closer to the two on the shore.

Mesmerised, the boy's eyes tracked the path of the flying visitor. Unblinking, he watched in awe as the fairy circled closer and closer. Wary of entering a relationship neither she nor the boy could have, she settled a few feet from the water's edge, looking at him.

The night grew cold, yet the boy would not leave. His forest companion stayed close by. The moon, playing host to the fairy's display, moved on.

A shadow from the far side of the lake signalled the fairy's departure. With one last sweep, she came to the edge of the lake and smiled at the still cold form of the boy.

It was morning when the boy's father found him; still sitting on the rock, cold and still, a smile on his frozen face. The Stag moved as the man arrived, but would not leave the boy.

There were two full moons that November, and, as for the first, the lake lay motionless in the moonlight.

At the appointed time, the water nymph flew across the lake, her wings dipping without a sound into the water with every beat. She flew to the rock where she had seen the boy. Coming to the spot, she stopped. Two sad eyes looked at her from the shore.

With a slow, sad nod of her head, she flew away, leaving the stag alone once more.

The Squire, the Farmer, and the Undine

Behind the thick wood, frequented only by forest animals, lay a large pond; too small for a lake, yet too large to be a pool. Water fed into the pond from a stream fed from high in the mountains to the north. Boulders and overhanging rocks edged the water, making access difficult, so dense there were few places where the animals could drink from the cool, fresh water.

The pond was the home of a solitary Undine, a water nymph. Each day she sat and watched the birds fly over the water or animals that came needing refreshment. By night she would sing; her voice was as pure as the mountain stream, as sweet as the perfume of the summer flowers that grew in clumps behind the rocks.

She longed to be whole. The Undine, perfect in every way, lacked one thing: a soul. She could never leave the pond unless it was to marry. The marriage would grant what she craved, but with the gift would come a terrible curse. Should her husband ever prove unfaithful, she would again return to the water, deprived of her hard-won soul while the unfaithful husband would die.

One night during a fierce storm, the local squire, lost after being thrown from his horse; captivated by the sweet sound of the Undine's voice, made his way to where she sat resting against a rock at the water's edge. The moonlight cast a soft glow onto her body, her eyes sparkled as if lit by starlight.

Mesmerised, he stood entranced by her visage until drawn by the melody and her beauty; lured, as sailors were by the sirens. His feet, with what seemed a mind of their own, transported him to where she sat.

"Who are you?" he asked, almost in a whisper.

Turning to face the intruder, she smiled. "I am who I am. But, should you wish it, I would become your wife, faithful unto death."

There, alone in the moonlight, he accepted her proposal. "Come then," he replied, "it shall be as you say."

"But wait, I must warn you," her eyes flashed with foreboding, "if you take me in marriage and ever prove unfaithful, you will die."

"That will never be," came his brave response.

Walking hand in hand, they made their way through the woods. At the nearest clearing, the squire's horse waited.

All the townsfolk attended the joyous wedding. As he slipped the gold band onto her finger, a soft breeze blew through the chapel. Her long tresses swayed as reeds by the water's edge bend to the unseen force. With eyes that danced to a new melody, her new soul arrived. Her love for the squire unchanged, but now a deeper, more primordial influence seeped through the nymph. She was now human.

His eyes were for her alone, and soon she was with child.

In a clearing, a little more than a mile from the pond, lived a farmer. His parents having died, he was the sole custodian of the land. Bonded to the squire from birth, he strove to be both loyal yet independent. Each year, he secured some of his crop and, as time went on, purchased several adjoining farms. Over the years, the squire and the farmer became familiar, but never friends.

As the time came for the Undine to be delivered of the baby, the squire arranged a grand celebration. Many of the towns-folk felt his endeavours presumptuous, and felt unease, though no one said a word. During the afternoon, the midwives, eager to ensure a clean and successful delivery, hovered around in the manor while he continued to prepare for the feast, oblivious to her struggling and pain in the upstairs bedroom.

The festivities were well under way when news reached the banqueting hall that a healthy baby boy had been born.

Content with her newborn, the Undine nursed the baby. The midwives fussed, happy the birth had brought no harm to the mother or child.

In the hall, mirth and liquor were much in abundance. All the farmers and servants drank the health of the squire, all except one. Sitting by himself, the farmer, though pleased at the squire's good fortune, both to be married and now having a son and heir, deep within his heart, harboured a gripping sadness. For he had in times past heard the nymph singing in the moonlight and often crept to the water's edge to see and hear her. His sorrow was that he had never found the courage to approach as she sat on the rock, never had he poured out his love for her and now, that could never be.

Late into the night's banquet, the squire, full of new wine, eyed a servant girl tending the tables. His abstinence from the pleasures of his wife, and with his morality clouded, took the girl to his chambers. In no position to refuse, he stripped her of her chastity in his drunken debauchery. His lust satisfied, he lay beside the defiled maid, and beside her, he died.

The breeze, which had brought in a sweet soul on her wedding day, now blew cold through the walls of the manor house. As news of her husband's death came to the Undine, a chill blast tore through her breast as she fed her newborn.

A short time following the funeral, the dead squire's brother arrived, announcing he would be the squire until the boy would come of age. When she repulsed his advances, he drove the Undine and her son from the estate.
Her soul now departed and now forced by the power of the curse; she headed back toward the pond. Passing the farmer's house, she stopped and knocked on the door. Pity filled his face as he saw her plight, though he knew not her fearful destiny. Pleading, she offered her son to his safe-keeping, telling him she must return to the water. With a nod and gentle outstretched arms, he took the boy from her grasp. From her heart, a sob was torn as she passed her child to another. Then, turning without a word, she disappeared into the wood.

Time passes, and time passed for the farmer and the boy. The child knew nothing of his mother, so assumed she had died at childbirth as mothers sometimes did. Together, they worked and played. Most evenings, they walked to the pond, where the farmer would take his lute and play melodies over the water.
Now and then, he would see the nymph. When he did, he would smile at her and play.
One night when the boy was approaching four years old, the moon being full, both were by the edge of the water. The farmer played while the boy laughed and danced. Helpless, she watched on, her grief beyond measure. Yet, in her agony, seeing her son dance in the moonlight to the gentle sounds of the lute, she once more broke out into the song of the water nymph.

The farmer and the boy stopped and listened; finding chords on his lute to match her lament. The three joined as one in the music and the moonlight.

"My heart is breaking, good sir. Seeing my son with you these nights is more than I can bear. Let me, as your maid, live by day in your house to cook and care for you and my son. By night I will return here. Would you show me now this second kindness? However," she cautioned him, "I will not lie with you, and should you force me, I will never return."

"You are most welcome," he replied.

Day by day, the Undine lived and worked at the farmer's side, but every evening after putting the boy to bed, returned to the water whence she came.

True to his word, the farmer never attempted to be with the Undine, though his heart ached for her company. At the end of each day, they would sit around the table. He would play and they would sing her songs, knowing she must soon leave, to return once more with the sunrise.

As things sometimes resolve with time, so it was for the Undine. The brother of the dead squire had neither wife nor bastard to carry on his name or rank; and during a harsh winter, he succumbed. The boy, now seven, was the only true and sole heir to the title. All the people knew it was the old squire's son who lived with the farmer, and so, at the behest of the village leaders, the farmer agreed to act as squire and guardian until the lad was of age.

The following morning, as the Undine prepared breakfast for the farmer and her son, he explained all that had transpired.

"I will not leave you," he told her.

"And I cannot go with you," came her pained reply.

"Yet," he moved closer to where she sat and took her hand, "as my wife, you would be bound to obey."

With his words still hanging in the air, a soft breeze blew off the water and her hair once again swayed as the new-leaved branches in spring. The love of the farmer, his loyalty, and devotion to her and hers to him, had broken the spell.

And so, the farmer, as principal landowner, became the new squire. With his now adopted son and heir, and new wife, they entered the manor.

Sons and daughters were born to the farmer and the nymph. All were beautiful, with voices to charm the hardest heart.

In happiness, they lived long and peaceful lives; she, now complete, her soul secure and he, her lord and husband, faithful unto death.

About the Author

Rob Clarke is a grey-haired engineer who sees
life through the eyes of a child. Sees knights and
dragons, struggling teenagers, the occasional
fairy, and a life worth striving for. His output
reflects on the madness of this world, yet hopes
to provide an escape into a land of dreams.
Novels, short stories and poetry form an eclectic
mix of philosophy, faith and fantasy; all seen
through the pen of a man who has long trod a
path less travelled.

Rob lives on the Mornington Peninsula, south of
Melbourne.

WEB: www.robclarke.com.au